Balancing Act

By

Meade Saeedi

ISBN 978-0-615-25423-4

Printed by Signature Book Printing,
www.sbpbooks.com

ACKNOWLEDGEMENTS

First, I thank literary agent David Morgan, who pointed out that a series of stories is not a novel, and taught me how to change one to the other.

Second, I appreciate the many times my writers group in Germantown patiently and repeatedly taught me style and emphasis.

And finally, I give great thanks to my friend Audrey Lynch who was instrumental in the final shaping of this novel.

To Phyllis,

Mark Speed

ONE

For the past five years, Sabrina Olensky had again lived on the edge of this small lake in northern Ohio, a place where she had spent her high school days but from which she had later divorced herself purposefully for decades. Her parents, Shirley and Wayne Newsome, had both died in this house, her mother fifteen years ago and her father nine years after that. Sabrina's mildly retarded younger sister Anna had lived here until the group home which Shirley Newsome fought so hard to establish finally opened in the mid 1980's.

Sabrina returned to this house shortly after the unexpected death of her husband, international trade negotiator Frank Olensky, which had been one of the major turning points of her life. For reasons she never quite understood, Sabrina had insisted on keeping this house even when no one in her family still lived here. Indeed, Sabrina stuck to this decision despite Frank's strenuous objections and her own sometimes paralyzing fears of the memories it held for her. Perhaps, she now considered, deep within herself she had somehow understood that she had to confront some very old demons of her own before she could begin to bridge the separation that had been growing between herself and her two still living children. Yes, perhaps, she thought, but oh, it was so difficult to allow those old, old memories to re-surface. She had hammered them down so hard, for so long.

Now, at the end of the final year of the twentieth century, Sabrina was facing another of life's turning points. She had finally decided to sell this big old house on the lake. It had become too time consuming and exhausting to mow the huge lawn, weed the five flower beds, and shovel the long driveway during harsh winters. Although she could have hired someone to see to these chores, Sabrina instead chose to accept a more manageable lifestyle for a woman approaching her sixties, and had therefore found herself a large condo home in a very desirable community nearby in Cleveland. She planned to move in January, which was just four months away.

The decision to move now forced Sabrina to face having to clean out the attic, a task she had assiduously avoided since her father's death. She had almost hired someone to come in and cart everything away, but at the last moment chose instead to go ahead and see what was still up there, as frightening as some of those memories might still be.

With a pretended sternness, she reprimanded herself. "You have to get this job done, so go ahead and do it. Nothing gets finished without first getting started." She chuckled to herself as she recalled how many times she had said those exact words to her children.

With re-formed resolve, Sabrina opened the attic door and flipped on the light. After the first two risers was a small landing before the staircase turned ninety degrees to the left and continued upward for another eight steps.

"Building codes sure were different back in the fifties," Sabrina mused as she noted that there were no handrails and the steps were exceptionally steep. "That's why the landing is now jammed with bundles of magazines, a crock pot, two suitcases and a drying rack. Dad just couldn't carry those things on to the top after he got into his eighties."

As she began to climb the steps, Sabrina was suddenly struck by a recurring memory that had troubled her so many times over the past five years. Collapsing on the landing, she knew full well that she couldn't stop herself from reliving it.

"Who gives this woman to be married to this man?" Reverend Olson asked, an unusual gentleness softening his normally booming voice.

Holding back the catch in her throat, Sabrina had answered clearly, even though her husband Frank had passed away only two months before. His death, resulting from a plane crash, occurred only a week before the originally planned wedding. Now on this bitterly cold November day, the rescheduled nuptials were finally taking place.

"Her late father and I do," she said, and with that confirmation, Sabrina had gently passed her eldest daughter along to the next phase of Karenna's life, noting sorrowfully that her child refused to meet Sabrina's eyes before stepping closer to the altar.

Attending the wedding had been Karenna's older brother, Paul, who was accompanied by his angry third wife. Also present were dozens of Frank's business associates from around the world, just as Frank had decreed it should be. Long time family friends from many communities where the Olensky's had lived across America also filled the pews to overflowing. In the back of everyone's minds, the memory of the deceased younger daughter Sarah remained an open sore. Beautiful Sarah, who had died years before at the age of only twenty-one. Karenna and Paul still partially blamed their mother for Sarah's death.

Sabrina shook her head as she arose, recalling how after Karenna's wedding she had been left to face her own life, one in which there was no husband to turn to (or from), no children to counsel, and only herself to rely upon. At that juncture in her life, she knew that she would dedicate her

energies to somehow restoring her remaining family's respect
for one another. However, at that time, she had no idea where
to begin. Sabrina had felt lost, alone, unappreciated and
unneeded.

Over the years, Sabrina had called Paul and Karenna
regularly, asking about their lives, inviting them to visit her in
Ohio, trying desperately to make her children understand that
she could still be part of their lives even though they were now
adults. Paul was the more vehement in rejecting his mother's
attempts, repeatedly saying that he was 'one messed up guy'
who now needed to sort out life on his own terms, although
he certainly had not been very successful in that endeavor,
Sabrina brooded. He had been married three times in less than
twelve years, with the third marriage on the rocks already.
Additionally, Paul had been jailed for drunk driving and
fired from most jobs because of difficulty controlling his hair
trigger temper. When Sabrina urged him to get counseling,
he laughed spitefully and reminded her how well that had
worked for him in the past. "No," he assured his mother, "no
therapist is ever going to mess with my head again," he told
her emphatically. "I'll sort out my own issues."

Karenna was just as successful at keeping their mother
out of her life. In the five years since the wedding, Sabrina
had never been invited to Texas to visit her daughter and son-
in-law, nor had Karenna ever come to the house by the lake

in Ohio. Indeed, Karenna made it clear that she preferred to spend her time in Chicago with Frank's mother. Nonetheless, Sabrina continued to call both children regularly, but the frozen feelings remained. Sabrina knew that there was always anger just under the surface, ready to spew out like molten lava at any moment.

Shaking her head and forcing herself back to the present, Sabrina blinked as she examined the present state of affairs on the landing. With a deep sigh, she carried everything down to the garage where she classified it either as junk or something to be recycled. Reluctantly, she returned to climb on up to the top of the steps.

When she arrived, Sabrina was fascinated by both the beauty and the chaos she observed. Cobwebs sieved the dust into intricate patterns behind the dim light of a forty watt bulb. Dust covered everything, almost like a warm blanket. Sabrina briefly regretted not wearing a face mask to protect her lungs, but decided against going back downstairs to find one. As she looked around, she noted how the attic was now littered with far more detritus than when she had last seen it many decades before. Ancient pieces of luggage, National Geographics from the eighties and nineties, old bedsprings and the empty boxes her mother saved for 'sometime when we might need them' now covered the floor all the way to the back of the attic. What worried Sabrina most, however, were the boxes filled with pictures, college keepsakes, and who knew what else. Sabrina knew that in some of them she would uncover reminders of the time when her life had been upended, totally ripped apart as though her existence had been forced relentlessly through a shredder.

Just as Sabrina was heading for a pile of boxes, the light bulb flickered and went out. Suddenly, darkness obscured everything and Sabrina was temporarily frozen in fear. Catching her breath, however, she carefully picked her way back to the front of the attic and followed the daylight which crept up the steps. Returning from the kitchen with a flashlight and a new seventy five watt bulb, she replaced the burned out light and immediately everything became visible.

Deciding to start with the empty boxes, she quickly looked through them to be sure there was nothing left inside by mistake. Finding no surprises, she carried them down to the discard pile in the garage and smashed them. Somehow that gave her a feeling of triumph, and she returned to the attic with even more vigor.

This time, Sabrina dragged one filled box to the center of the attic where she could see clearly and heaved it up onto a table. Cautiously, she unfolded the flaps. There was a yellowed newspaper covering the contents. Sabrina looked for a date and found it, July 14, 1959. That was the summer her family had moved to this house. Apparently, this box had never even been unpacked, but had somehow come straight to the attic. Intrigued, Sabrina wondered what it could be.

Slowly she removed the newspaper and found a large number of objects of roughly the same size. *This is almost like Christmas*, she thought with delight. Briefly, Sabrina recalled how her mother had always insisted that everyone try to speculate what a gift might be before opening it, which had led to many hilarious wrong guesses and lots of laughing on holidays and birthdays. She sighed as she recalled those happy memories, then cautiously picked up the topmost package and tried to surmise what it was from the feel. Solid and heavy, almost like a paperweight. But it was oblong and had appendages. She gave up conjecturing and rapidly opened it. When she finally recognized what she had found, Sabrina actually squealed with delight. She was staring at her collection of horse statues that had never been found after their move.

Slowly, she unwrapped each one, recalling the names she had given each statue as she stroked a ceramic nose or gently rearranged plastic legs. Chocolate had been her favorite horse at the summer camp she attended for six years. Her eyes teared as she remembered how heartbroken she had been one summer when the camp director tried to explain as kindly as possible that Chocolate had reared in fright during a thunderstorm the previous winter and struck his head on a barn support, dying instantly. Sabrina had purchased this statue in Chocolate's memory. Next she found the ceramic mare and foal statue she had selected in hopes that her own horse, bought for her when she was in the fourth grade to compensate for serious medical problems she was facing, would someday have a baby. Despite many attempts at breeding, however, that had never happened. Then there was the trotter and sulky to remind her of all the summers she had spent at the fairgrounds, walking race horses to cool them down after the local races.

Sabrina continued unwrapping until her whole collection stood in front of her, all thirty five statues. She gazed at her treasures lovingly, wondering if she would be able to find somewhere to put them in her new home. Eventually she chose to make that decision later, since right now she could not bear to consider parting with them again, after all the time she had thought they were lost.

Next she opened an antique trunk, now more than one hundred years old. It had once brought clothes and china and other valued possessions into her grandparents' home, and had later been a wedding present to Wayne and Shirley when they were married in 1941. Inside Sabrina found fine white linen tablecloths that were now yellowed with age. "Probably the trash can for those," she murmured regretfully, "unless there's a way to restore aged linens. I'll have to find out." Beneath the linens lay an exquisite set of eight crystal glasses.

Sabrina looked at them admiringly, then reluctantly admitted that she would probably sell these, since she had no significant emotional attachment to them.

By the time she had finished sorting out everything in the trunk, she realized it was late afternoon. Greatly relieved that nothing truly frightening had been found on her first day in the attic, Sabrina decided that it was time to stop.

Gratefully, she descended the stairs. In the kitchen, she automatically looked for the clock that had been above the sink since she was ten years old. Of course, it wasn't there. Her father had removed it soon after his wife died, but even though Sabrina had lived in this house for five years now, she somehow couldn't remember that it was gone.

Earlier in the week, Sabrina had agreed to meet her friend Sally for dinner at six thirty that evening. Deciding that she still had time for a nice long soak in the tub, Sabrina dropped her dirty clothes by the washer in the laundry room, then ran herself a tub of wonderfully hot water. She poured in bubble bath, arranged her bath pillow and slowly lowered herself into the warm elixir, sighing peacefully as comfort permeated her tired body. She flipped through a magazine that she kept by the tub until she began to feel sleepy, then scrunched down a little further into the water and closed her eyes, languidly dropping the magazine on the floor. In a moment, she was snoring gently, with her head lolling against the comforting pillow.

Far away, she heard a jangling, which awakened her slightly. The telephone, she realized. Well, that was what answering machines were for, so a person could nap in the tub at the end of a hard day of sorting out memories. She lay there until the water finally began to cool, then pulled the stopper up with her toes, just as she had when she was a child. The water sputtered out, and Sabrina reluctantly stood up, showered off and stepped out onto the thick bath mat. When she returned to her bedroom, she glanced at the phone but decided not to listen to the message. Then realizing that it might be Sally with an emergency, she played it back. In utter astonishment, Sabrina listened to a voice she had not heard for nearly four decades.

"Hello, Cara Mia." The voice sounded so warm. "I am in America for a few weeks. I will call you again later. I still love you."

Sabrina replayed the message four times, savoring the sound of Francisco's voice. Francisco, the man who had taught her both the sweetness and the passion of love, and whose heart she had one day mangled, telling herself that it had to be that way. After so many years, how could he possibly still invoke such strong feelings in her heart, she wondered in bewilderment. Shaking her head, she chided herself for reacting like an infatuated teenager, rather than a woman nearly sixty years old. "Ignore it," she told herself angrily. "Let the past remain where it is. There's no way you can rekindle what you and Francisco had. You destroyed that trust long ago. Now just let it be."

She forced the call out of her mind and dressed casually for dinner. Just as she was going out the front door, the phone rang again. She paused for a second, then walked on out and closed the door behind her.

Driving into town, perhaps a little faster than usual, Sabrina pulled into one of the few remaining parking spaces at Larky's. A crazy name, she thought, but the restaurant was very popular because it had both wonderful food and a funky atmosphere. Sally and Sabrina enjoyed eating here at least twice a month, ever since the two women had met at an American Association of University Women meeting soon after Sabrina moved back to Ohio. Sabrina recalled wistfully that AAUW was one of the associations she had always meant to join while she was married, but meeting times inevitably conflicted with family obligations. Now, however, time was almost entirely her own to do with as she pleased.

Sally was already seated in a booth at the rear of the restaurant, looking very secretive as Sabrina joined her. Immediately Sabrina asked, almost with trepidation, "OK, cat that swallowed the canary. What is it?"

Sally grinned mischievously and answered, "How about a little adventure, totally unplanned, starting tomorrow?"

"Uh, oh," was Sabrina's response. "The last time you planned an adventure, we ended up snorkeling in water with no fish, and I got a miserable burn on my back."

Sally laughed uproariously. "Well," she assured her skeptical friend. "this one is really great. No water. Just two nights at a casino in Atlantic City, plus air fare and ground transportation, all for $69."

"What?" Sabrina gasped. That was unbelievable. These days, sixty-nine dollars would hardly get you to Toledo by bus.

"Yup. $69."

"Where did you hear about it?" Sabrina still did not believe it.

"It was advertised in the newspaper. You must have missed it."

"Tomorrow, really?"

Sally pulled out two tickets. "I thought you'd be interested."

"You know," Sabrina mused, "an old boyfriend of mine once told me that if he could take me anywhere in America, it would be Atlantic City. Of course, that was back in the sixties, when Atlantic City was just a boardwalk town with an annual beauty pageant, and I guess he thought it was a lovely place. He was from Peru and probably hadn't traveled much around the good old US of A."

"Actually, he was probably right," Sally answered. "Atlantic City was a big tourist draw a long time ago. It was where all the wealthy people spent their summers. You know, don't you, that the properties on the original Monopoly board were named for streets in Atlantic City."

"You're kidding." Sabrina really was surprised. "Well, maybe he knew something I didn't."

"He sounds smart to me," Sally quipped. "Whatever happened to him?"

This time Sabrina answered very slowly. "My parents opposed the relationship, especially my mother."

"Un, oh. That's always a problem," Sally responded sympathetically. "How old were you?"

"Freshman in college. First love. They told me I would get over it."

"Did you?" Sally was becoming intrigued.

"No." Sabrina was startled at how quickly that answer burst out of her mouth. Perhaps it had come directly from her heart, she realized.

"So, what happened?"

Sabrina hesitated, then finally managed to say, "Some problems came up, and eventually, he went back to Lima and married someone else. A few years later, I married Frank."

"What kind of problems?" Sally probed.

"I don't want to remember." Sabrina's face became a mask.

This had happened before during conversations about Sabrina's personal life, and Sally knew better than to push. Still, she wanted her friend to get the anguish out into the open so that it no longer haunted her.

"Whenever you're ready to talk about it, my ears are open."

Unfortunately, Sally was offering to be a true friend, but Sabrina was not yet ready to have one.

TWO

Following a lengthy dinner marked by both giggles and occasional extended silences, Sabrina and Sally agreed to meet at Cleveland Hopkins Airport early the next morning. That night, Sabrina tried to get to sleep early, but instead tossed restlessly for hours as long suppressed memories from childhood continually invaded her consciousness. When she finally slipped off to sleep, Sabrina began to hear her mother talking in that authoritative manner that had caused Sabrina such anguish as a child

*   *   *

"Sabrina, darling, it's time to get ready for roller skating."

Twelve year old Sabrina Newsome scrunched her eyes into nothingness and ground her teeth until her jaw hurt. She was sick and tired of being obedient. Every Friday night she had to go roller skating with Patty, that stuck up snob who was super popular with the rest of the kids at school. She and Patty used to be friends, but not anymore. Did her mother care? No, her mother still insisted on arranging a zillion activities together because Patty was part of the in-crowd, and Sabrina no longer was.

"I'm not feeling good, Mom. Bad headache," Sabrina responded grouchily. "I want to stay home tonight." To herself she grumbled, "Why can't the magnificent Shirley Newsome leave her daughter alone for just one single solitary night? Let me play records in my room or read a book, just for once. That's all I want. Just one night for me to choose how I spend my time, not her." Nonetheless, Sabrina knew she had little chance of winning. Her mother always won.

A playground accident four years earlier had left Sabrina with one arm permanently misaligned, so she now not only looked odd but was physically inept as well. Suddenly, the child who had once been the champion athlete and everybody's best friend had become a social outcast as her personality had changed from positive strength to angry defensiveness.

"Come on, Sweetheart," her mother called again from downstairs. "You need exercise, and besides, you don't want all those skating lessons to go to waste, do you? You can show Patty that new turnaround you learned last week. And Bobby might be there."

Sabrina was not yet sophisticated enough to realize that her artful mother knew this was an inducement Sabrina could not resist. Bobby was older, a sophomore in high school from a different district. He and his twin brother Jack came to the rink almost every Friday night. A few weeks before, unknown to Sabrina, Shirley had stopped the boys as they were coming off the floor and persuaded them to ask Sabrina and Patty to skate one dance with them. Acquiescing to Shirley's charm, they had readily agreed, and each week since then the two boys invited Sabrina and Patty for at least one waltz around the rink.

Therefore, with a sigh of resignation, Sabrina yanked on her skating skirt and glared at herself in the mirror, moaning again that she wasn't allowed to wear lipstick, even though most of her classmates did. By now, the disgust engendered by the ugliness of her grotesquely bent arm was buried so deep that she no longer recognized that as the source of her constant disquietude. Instead, her anger was directed at things like lipstick and her mother's old fashioned attitudes. When she clunked down the stairs, deliberately banging her skating case against the banister, she muttered, "OK, I'm ready. Let's go."

"Just a second, honey. I have to be sure Gata is okay."

Sabrina groaned at yet another of her mother's annoying eccentricities. Whenever they left the house, her mother had to hunt everywhere to be sure the family cat had not slipped out the door or gotten caught somewhere. In high dudgeon, Sabrina stomped back up the steps and started looking through all the rooms. "She's under your bed," she announced a minute later. "Now, let's go."

"Are you sure you saw her?"

"Are you calling me a liar?" Sabrina shouted down the stairs, egregious pain in her voice. "Come look for yourself if you don't believe me."

Her mother did just that, then collected the keys and headed for the car.

Once in the car, Sabrina began needling her mother, demanding an answer to the same question she asked every time her mother drove over to Patty's house. "Why can't Patty's mother ever drive? How come you always have to do it?" she insisted.

Exerting enormous patience, Shirley Newsome replied calmly, "I've told you that Mrs. Williams doesn't have a driver's license. Besides, sweetheart, I'm your mother. I don't mind doing anything for you. Whatever you need, I'm here to help because I love you. You are my precious daughter, Sabrina."

Indeed, Shirley Newsome did take motherhood seriously. When Sabrina's social status changed after the accident,

Shirley immediately developed an ambitious plan of action. She invited a select group of Sabrina's most socially desirable classmates over to the house on Saturday afternoons and taught them how to bake fancy cookies, which was one of Shirley's special talents. Next she became a co-leader of the Girl Scout troop and began taking the girls on exotic trips to earn unusual badges. Suddenly Sabrina's mom had become everyone's surrogate mother, listening attentively to pre-teen angst and doling out advice which made wonderful sense to all Sabrina's classmates, although rarely to Sabrina.

Unfortunately, Sabrina paid a high price for her mother's anxiety. The more her mother tried to befriend classmates on Sabrina's behalf, the more Sabrina became infuriated at how the other girls thought her mom was so great, while Sabrina herself resented every suggestion Shirley made. As Sabrina became more confused, her mother became more domineering, and the entwining circle continued to tighten as both accomplices accelerated toward a storm that would one day go far beyond what either of them could ever have contemplated.

During the five minute ride to Patty's house, Sabrina leveled a new volley. "How come Anna doesn't have to get exercise? How come she can stay home when I have to go skating? Anna needs exercise, too, you know. And when are we going to get a television? Everyone else at school has one. Daddy makes lots of money. You and he are always talking about buying a new sofa or something, so why not a television?"

At this, Shirley set her mouth in that way mothers do when they have been sassed one too many times, even though she felt her heart twang. Indeed, Shirley did strive to meet Anna's needs just as rigorously as she tried to do everything right for Sabrina. As the primary caretaker for two special needs children because her husband was tied up with his many business activities all the time, Shirley was constantly frazzled beyond exhaustion, but nonetheless still insisted on being super mom every day.

"So, why can't we have a television?" Sabrina persisted. "A couple of years ago you went over to the Johnson's to watch those Senate hearings about communism, or whatever they were. If you can watch TV, why can't I?"

"The McCarthy hearings were a matter of national importance," Shirley answered with yet more deliberate patience. "But most shows on television are just silly things. There are plenty of better ways for a bright young woman like you to spend your time."

"You let me go over to Patty's and watch Wonderful World of Disney. There are plenty of cool shows like that."

Shirley had had it. "Enough," was all she had to say. The tone let Sabrina know that she was one word away from losing her allowance. Nothing more was said until they arrived at Patty's house. Sabrina let up for the moment, but knew that she would continue to fight back against her feelings of impotence some other way, some other time.

Upon arriving at Patty's house, Sabrina and Patty climbed into the rear seat of the station wagon, which faced backwards so the passengers could see oncoming traffic. It was the 'in' model of the year, and Shirley had coerced Wayne into buying it as an incentive for Sabrina's classmates to agree to go places with her.

In the front seat, Shirley prepared herself for another interminable evening of listening to Patty's mother's problems. Last week they had talked about Tamara's unsuccessful attempts to lose weight, and the week before had been a story of a feud with the next door neighbor over the neighbor's yapping dogs. Shirley had observed that Tamara mother was very effective at describing problems, but never seemed to be able to come up with solutions.

When they arrived at the skating rink, Shirley pulled up to the entrance so Sabrina and Patty would not have to walk across the parking lot. The girls got out carelessly, banging their cases against the side of the station wagon. Shirley did not say anything, but she knew that Wayne would be furious if he saw a dent. "Watch for moving cars," she cautioned, but Patty and Sabrina were already gone.

After finding a space large enough for the station wagon, the mothers walked inside and headed for the observation deck overlooking the rink itself. Live music was provided by an organist, who just then was performing a Buddy Holly song, *Peggy Sue*. The skaters skimmed happily around the rink as Shirley and Tamara watched.

"I think I see some of the girls' classmates," Shirley noted, but Tamara just nodded her head and did not bother to give a verbal response. After a few minutes, two other girls rolled over to chat with Patty and Sabrina. Soon they took off, Patty in tow. Sabrina got up and bravely began to skate around the rink on her own, then slid back to the benches and sat down, her head hanging. Then just as quickly, she was back on the floor, skating smoothly and waving nonchalantly at the other girls as she passed them by. *She's a tough kid*, Shirley thought admiringly. *Somehow, she's going to be okay*.

After several one word responses from Tamara as Shirley made more attempts to begin a conversation, Shirley finally suggested, "How about if we stop at Isaly's for an ice cream on the way home tonight?"

"Oh, all right. I guess I can afford the calories," Tamara replied grudgingly. Shirley smiled to herself, knowing full well that stopping for ice cream was one of Tamara's favorite activities. Appreciating that for once Tamara was not plying her with lots of petty concerns, Shirley decided to relax and just enjoy tonight's respite from problem solving. She watched the skaters below as she allowed herself a short amount of non troubled time.

It did not last long. Tamara had gone downstairs to call Patty over to the side, and Shirley knew trouble was brewing. When Shirley reached to bottom of the steps, Patty was whining loudly at her mother. "But Mom, it'll be ladies' choice after just two more songs, and I wanted to ask Jack like I always do. Why do you have to go NOW?"

Unsure what to do, Tamara looked at Shirley, who stepped in quickly, "Why don't we stay for another fifteen minutes, then we'll stop at Isaly's for a sundae. How does that sound, Patty?"

As Shirley had anticipated, Patty was delighted with the intervention on her behalf. "Super, Mrs. N. Thanks a lot." Off Patty flew, while Tamara turned red from embarrassment that she could not handle the situation herself.

Shortly thereafter, Patty found Jack and Sabrina found Bobby for the ladies choice dance. Soon they were skating to the Tennessee Waltz, and Bobby was supporting Sabrina as she skated backward. As sometimes happened, Sabrina allowed her mind to slip into one of her daydreams about being popular again, and a smile spread across her face.

"What are you thinking about? It sure seems to make you happy." Bobby's question snapped Sabrina's attention back to where she was.

"Oh, nothing," she stammered as a blush crept up her neck and suffused her whole face. "I'm just enjoying the skating."

"I don't think so. I think you were thinking about something really nice." Then Sabrina noticed that Bobby was looking at her in a way she had not seen before. "Do you go out on dates?" he asked suddenly.

Sabrina was instantly flustered. "No, I'm not allowed," she answered quickly. "I only go to school things with my classmates. Dances, band recitals, you know, stuff like that." Now Sabrina felt really stupid and wished she could just sink into the floor and disappear.

"How would you like to go the movies with me?" Bobby persisted.

Astonished, Sabrina mumbled. "I don't think I could," she said. "I mean, my parents wouldn't allow it."

Bobby was ready with a suave answer. "They wouldn't have to know. Just say you're going somewhere with a girlfriend." Now he put his hand in the middle of her back and pulled her a little closer.

"Ah, thanks, but I don't think so," Sabrina managed to say. Then suddenly she tripped backwards, landing on her bad arm and causing the pain to shoot straight up to her eyeballs.

"Oh, let me help you up," Bobby crooned, the epitome of concern. He scooped his arm under Sabrina and carried her over to the benches. By the time they got there, Shirley was running toward her daughter.

"She's all right, Ma'am," Bobby reassured the terrified Mrs. Newsome. "I think she just jarred herself a bit."

"Thank you Bobby," Shirley said indistinctly as she directed her concern only toward her daughter. "Are you all right, darling? Let me look. Does anything hurt?"

Bobby interrupted. "I'd like to give you my phone number, Ma'am. Then Sabrina could call me to tell me that she's all right." Behind Shirley's back, he winked at Sabrina. Without waiting for Shirley's permission, he handed Sabrina a piece of paper folded in half. No one noticed that he already had his phone number written down, even before Sabrina's fall.

After determining that nothing was broken, Shirley canceled plans to stop at Isaly's, took Patty and her mother directly home, then headed straight for the emergency room at the nearest hospital. When Sabrina was pronounced fine by the physician on duty, they finally drove home. While her mother was looking away, Sabrina slipped Bobby's telephone number into her treasure drawer and vowed that she would call him as soon as she had a chance.

*   *   *

Sabrina rolled over, almost awake, but not quite. She tried to remember what she had been dreaming about, but could not. She kicked at her covers, plumped her pillow several times, then fell back asleep.

*   *   *

The opportunity to call Bobby presented itself just a few nights later. Because Sabrina's parents had given her a telephone of her own for her twelfth birthday and had even installed a connection for it in Sabrina's bedroom, she had a modicum of privacy when she wanted to make a call, but only if her mother were not there to tell her what to say. So when Shirley and Wayne were obliged to attend a Rotary Club function the following Wednesday evening, Sabrina knew this was her chance to call Bobby and speak privately.

The housemaid, Eugenia, was staying that night to take care of the girls while Shirley and Wayne were away for the evening. When Eugenia announced, 'bedtime in ten minutes,' for once Sabrina did not put up a fuss. Knowing that Eugenia enjoyed listening to a religious program at night, Sabrina listened carefully until she heard the click of the radio being turned on. When she heard the low drone of the preacher's voice, she knew it would then be safe to call Bobby.

With her trusty Girl Scout flashlight in hand, she pulled the telephone under the covers and nervously began to dial the number. Realizing she had reversed two of the digits, she hung up and began again. Sabrina took a deep breath and closed her eyes as the phone began to ring. However, just as someone picked it up, Sabrina heard a loud thump, thump, thump coming from Anna's room next door. Slamming the phone down, she untangled herself from her bedcovers and joined Eugenia in a flight down the hall. When they pushed open the door to Anna's room, they were astounded to see Anna bouncing a baseball against the wall and trying to catch it in a mitt that was way too big for her tiny hand.

Sabrina was outraged. "That's my baseball glove, Horseface," she bellowed, while trying to rip the glove off her sister's hand. "How dare you steal it out of my room?"

Anna threw the ball again, and Eugenia deftly picked it out of the air. Anna began sobbing as Sabrina continued to reclaim her glove, still yelling at her sister. "Give it back, *now*. And don't you ever *dare* take anything out of my room again."

Eugenia separated the sisters before a serious ruckus began, and when it all got settled out, each girl grumpily went back to bed as Eugenia heaved a sigh of relief.

Again Sabrina waited until she was sure Eugenia was listening to her program before dialing Bobby's number. This time it was busy. After two more attempts, the call finally went through. By then, it was almost ten o'clock. Bobby's mother answered on the sixth ring.

"Hi, is Bobby home, please," Sabrina managed to get out, nearly stuttering over her own words.

"Honey, do you want Junior or Senior?" Bobby's mother asked. Sabrina wasn't sure, and asked for Junior. The person who came to the phone sounded older than her father.

"Uh, I'm trying to reach the Bobby who goes to the skating rink on Friday nights," she babbled.

"Oh, that one. We call him Robert around here, just to keep him separate from Gramps and me. Hold on a minute." To the side, Sabrina heard, "Hey, Robert, it's another one of your skating rink pick ups."

What seemed like an eternity later, Bobby came to the phone. "Yeah?"

"Hi, Bobby," Sabrina said bravely. "This is Sabrina. I just wanted to let you know that my arm is better. Hope I'm not calling too late."

"Oh, Sabrina. Good, I'm glad you called," Bobby crooned. "Hey, I was just thinking. How about if you meet me at the theater down on Market Street Saturday afternoon. We'll take in a good movie, and I'll buy you some popcorn."

Sabrina had been half hoping he would ask her for a date, and three quarters hoping he wouldn't. She tried to respond in as grown up a manner as possible. "Sorry. I couldn't make it Saturday afternoon because my Mom has a bunch of my classmates over to our house for a baking lesson." Yeah, real grown up, Sabrina groaned to herself, realizing that she sounded like a fool. However, she kept on trying. "I could make it during the week, though, maybe Thursday."

'Thursday?" Bobby muttered. "Why Thursday? How could you get there without being missed?'

"I'm supposed to meet some friends to go to the shopping center that day after school. It's one of the rare times when my Mom isn't right on top of me. Instead of meeting them, I could meet you."

"Well, all right then. I'll meet you Thursday at half past four. Market Street Theater,'" Bobby agreed. "Now I have to run. See ya."

"OK. Bye now," Sabrina answered. "I'll be there."

After hanging up, Sabrina stared at her telephone in astonishment. She couldn't believe that she had actually made a date, and her parents didn't know a thing about it. It was the first secretive thing she had ever done. Her feelings of satisfaction overcame the anxiety of having been duplicitous.

That Thursday morning, Sabrina passed a note to Patty during math class. 'Can't go shopping with you this PM. Sorry.' Patty turned around and gave Sabrina a 'who cares' look as she crumpled the note.

At four thirty-five, Sabrina was standing in front of the theater, starting to worry that she had been stood up. Then she saw Bobby coming away from the ticket counter, and she breathed a small sigh of relief.

"I got tickets to *Rebel Without a Cause*," Bobby announced, as if he had done something spectacular. Although it was the only show available, he was trying to impress Sabrina, since he had overheard her talking about James Dean at the rink. "Come on, let's get something to eat."

He plied her with a Coke, buttered popcorn, and a large box of Milk Duds, saying that it was a long movie and he didn't want her to get hungry. Then they stood outside the movie entrance as they waited for the previous showing to let out.

Suddenly, Sabrina saw one of her classmates coming around the corner. It was Mike, a loudmouth who delighted in finding fault with everyone but himself. She tried to duck behind a telephone booth, but didn't make it in time.

"Well, hello, Miss Newsome," he declared, walking up to her and Bobby, placing great emphasis on the Miss. "Does your Mommy know that you're running around with high school boys?"

"This is my cousin, from Atlanta," Sabrina blurted out.

Mike looked Bobby up and down, then smirked. "Funny, he looks just like a boy who tried to get smart with my sister once. The name was Robert. My dad beat the tar out of him."

"Come on, Sabrina. Let's go on in to the movie," Bobby said, sweat beginning to sheen on his forehead as he pulled her in through the outstreaming moviegoers.

"I think I'll give your Mommy a call," Mike called out, "before you get home, so be prepared for a great reception. Where did you tell her you were going -- shopping with girlfriends?" Mike guffawed as he disappeared out of the theater.

Sabrina was sure she was in the deepest pit ever dug by a twelve year old girl, utterly convinced that she would never see daylight again. She and Bobby held hands during the movie, but throughout the entire show, she was trying desperately to come up with a reasonable explanation for her parents. When the show was over, Bobby refused to ride the bus back with her, saying he had somewhere else to go. Sabrina was terrified to go home, but couldn't think of anywhere else to go, aside from running away permanently. She reluctantly discarded that thought, since she had just three dollars with her.

"What am I going to say?" she asked him plaintively.

"You're smart. You'll come up with a good story," Bobby assured her, as he headed the opposite direction. "Maybe I'll see you tomorrow night at the rink," he added, all the while vowing to himself that he would never go near that skating rink again.

Sabrina rode the bus home, walked two blocks to her house, and slowly opened the front door, fully expecting the world to crash in on her. Perhaps her mother had already called the police. She looked back outside, but didn't see a cruiser anywhere.

Hi," she called tentatively. "I'm back."

Nothing happened. Her mother asked what she had bought, and Sabrina lamely answered that she hadn't seen anything she liked.

"That's fine, dear. You don't have to buy something every time you go shopping. Now go wash your hands. It's time for dinner."

Sabrina finally let out her breath, deciding that maybe there was a God after all. She didn't fight with her mother over anything that night.

Two years later, when Sabrina was in junior high, Shirley heard about a medical procedure that had successfully restored function to permanently damaged limbs. She consulted several local orthopedic surgeons and learned that the new surgery was highly risky and could result in even further nerve damage. This did not deter Shirley. Not satisfied with the opinions of local doctors, she went to the Cleveland Clinic and spoke with specialists there. Still not satisfied, she called the surgeon in New York who had pioneered the procedure. After months of investigation, Shirley was convinced that there was a substantial possibility that Sabrina could look normal again, and she discussed it with Wayne.

To Shirley's perplexity, Wayne was totally opposed. "Are you crazy?" he demanded. "That child has already spent more time in hospitals and doctors' offices than any fifty kids we know put together. Why would you even think of creating more misery for her?"

"I'm not creating misery," Shirley had responded angrily. "I'm offering hope. Wayne, I've spent two months investigating this possibility. How dare you just reject it out of hand?"

Sabrina walked into the house just at the end of the conversation. "Investigating what?' she asked, knowing that her parents seldom fought over anything other than what was best for her and Anna.

Shirley responded first. "Come in and sit down, Sabrina." Her mother's voice was so formal, Sabrina was on guard immediately.

"What's going on?" Sabrina asked, starting to feel scared. Shirley picked up on her daughter's emotions immediately.

"There's nothing for you to be frightened about," Shirley said soothingly. "Daddy and I were talking about something that might help you, that's all."

"Like what?" Sabrina demanded angrily. When her parents both started thinking up things that were good for her, it usually meant another afternoon lesson of some kind.

"Would you like to have your arm look like everyone else's again?" her mother asked.

Sabrina was thunderstruck. "Of course," she sputtered. "That's a really dumb question. But that's never going to happen, so why are you even talking about it?"

"Well, Sabby," her father interjected, deciding to present a united front with his wife, "your mother has been talking to some doctors, and they think maybe they can do something for you. But there is no one hundred per cent guarantee, and it might not work."

Sabrina was sitting up very straight by then. "What do you mean, 'something could be done'? Could they actually straighten this arm out and make it so I could hold books and open doors and do things everyone else does?" Pausing for a second, she asked hesitantly, "Could I actually be normal again?" The look of hope in her eyes tore at the hearts of both her parents.

"Daddy and I will discuss it, then we'll all three sit down and make a decision," Shirley answered.

Sabrina doubted that her opinion would really be taken into consideration. It never was when both her parents were involved. Nonetheless, she went to her room, her head filled with dreams of being able to play on the basketball team the following season.

In the end, both parents agreed to risk the surgery. Wayne was impressed with the thoroughness of Shirley's research, and he wanted more than anything to have his daughter be accepted, not only now as a child in school, but more importantly, in the adult world that lay ahead of her.

Shirley and Sabrina went to New York City over spring break, but nothing was said to anyone outside the family. Having had a hard enough time with Wayne, Shirley did not want to deal with negative opinions from concerned but uninformed friends and neighbors.

Sabrina had been in hospitals many times before. However, this was the first time she had ever taken anesthesia, and the experience was terrifying. Ether was used, dripped through a gauze mask. It created strange images in Sabrina's head, as she kept seeing a huge fat-faced clown zinging around and around on a circular track. Every time the clown came looming near, she saw a horrible grin and smelled an awful odor. That memory remained with her for the rest of her life, resulting in her feeling nauseous whenever she had to fill the gas tank.

The surgery lasted for several hours, and Sabrina's arm was immobilized for four days thereafter. It was an agonizing time for everyone, but finally on the fifth day the restraints were removed.

Looking in the mirror, Sabrina instantly saw that the permanently dislocated appearance of her arm had been remedied, and she gave a small sigh of relief. The real test, however, would be to see if it moved properly. Sabrina mentally commanded her limb to move. At first, the decree did not seem to be understood by the muscles, then gradually, a little at a time, her arm began to move back and forth.

For a moment, no one said anything, not even Shirley. She looked at her daughter, for once acknowledging Sabrina's right to speak first.

Suddenly, Sabrina was crying ferociously. "Thank you, Dr. Goodman, thank you," she managed to get out. Then she said the words that brought her mother to tears.

"And thank you, Mommy."

Shirley had not heard the word Mommy from Sabrina's lips for years, just as she had not heard a thank you for nearly as long. Tears welled in her eyes, and she hugged Sabrina tenderly, all the while gazing at Dr. Goodman in absolute gratitude. "God bless you," she mouthed to the doctor as she rocked her restored child in her arms. "Thank you beyond words."

*   *   *

Again, Sabrina rolled over and this time she finally fell into a deep unencumbered sleep.

THREE

The alarm jolted Sabrina awake at six thirty the next morning. Arising sluggishly, she felt slightly disoriented until she remembered the upcoming trip to Atlantic City, which instantly focused her on preparing for what she hoped would be thoroughly enjoyable holiday.

When she arrived at the terminal, she stopped by the Pretzel Emporium to treat herself to their cinnamon covered special, then stood next to the magazine rack where she and Sally had agreed to rendezvous. A moment later, Sally breathlessly arrived, grumbling about traffic, then extracting a promise from Sabrina as they walked toward their runway.

"In all these years, she said, "you never told me how you and Frank met and fell in love. During the flight today, I want to hear all about it."

Blanching, Sabrina mumbled a vague reply about a convoluted story that would take too long to tell.

"I mean it," Sally persisted. "I've drilled your head full of stories about Ted and me, our kids, stupid things we've done, even Ted's funeral. Now it's your turn to unload on me."

"Okay," Sabrina answered indistinctly. "Maybe one hour will be enough to tell you part of the story, at least." She then became quiet as she searched her mind about what she would and would not tell her friend. Eventually, when they were in the air, she recounted parts of her childhood, especially the ongoing contest between herself and her mother for control over her life. To her surprise, Sabrina found herself admitting to Sally that she still felt bewildered by her conflicting emotions toward her mother.

"As I was raising my own children," Sabrina acknowledged, "I would frequently berate myself for not appreciating how many trials mothers endure. On the other hand, I always felt a bitter resentment over the frustration her domination still somehow engendered, even after I had become a parent myself. Sometimes I felt helpless to cope with my children's issues, as if I had to ask for help with even minor problems. That was when I really became angry. At times like that, I believed that my mother had totally stripped me of self confidence."

She then began to tell Sally about the regime she endured during late elementary school and junior high, as her mother worked hard to re-integrate Sabrina into the social fabric of a pre-teen world.

"One day after school," Sabrina began, "I would have a music lesson so that I would be first chair French horn player in the school band. The next day would be a 'social arts' class with some old biddy who told me how to hold a teacup and create a proper conversation."

"What's wrong with that?" Sally asked. "I haven't heard anything yet that hurt you." Sally had expected to hear a love story about the romance between Sabrina and Frank, not a recital of pre-teen angst.

"I had no choice," Sabrina complained. "Then there were the nightly spelling drills with my mother so I could win the school spelling bee every year. Actually, I did win the state championship in seventh grade and got to go to Washington DC to compete in the national finals," Sabrina added with a touch of pride.

"So?" Sally was beginning to get a bit put out with Sabrina's complaints about nothing.

"I guess all that was nothing extraordinary, just a parent trying to help her child," Sabrina finally admitted. "But the most difficult thing for me was the Friday nights at the skating rink, where I had to go with Patty, even though I couldn't stand being around her anymore, after she changed from my best friend to the kid who was meanest to me all the time. At the skating rink was where I met this older boy, Bobby, who was a really good skater."

Sabrina was about to tell Sally about the debacle at the movie theater when suddenly the seatbelt light flashed on and the pilot announced that they were approaching a patch of severe turbulence. He instructed the flight attendants to discontinue beverage service and passengers to return to their seats immediately. Suddenly the plane bucked and passengers began screaming hysterically. A passenger who had earlier been refused another alcoholic drink because of his obnoxious behavior began cursing loudly and threatening to sue the airline for every penny it had. Children screamed and one fell into the aisle because the mother had tried holding the child herself rather than obeying instructions to fasten his seat belt. Debris flew everywhere and people were shrieking after being burned by spilled coffee. A woman who had been applying makeup stabbed herself in the eye with her mascara brush.

Sabrina and Sally endured as best they could while their heads whacked against the backs of their seats. The misery seemed to last forever, then the furor was suddenly over and the plane returned to smooth flight. Two flight attendants immediately went to the aid of several injured passengers as well as a fellow stewardess who had not been able to get back to her seat in time and was now lying in the aisle groaning, having bounced off the ceiling when the plane hit an air pocket.

Sally was thoroughly terrified. "Oh, God, I'm never going to fly again," she wailed as she looked around at the destruction caused by the short furor. Cups were strewn everywhere, their former contents now staining the clothes of most passengers, and children were still crying hysterically.

"It's going to be okay," Sabrina reassured her friend. "We're almost there." Then she realized that she had smacked her nose into the back of the seat in front of her and it was oozing blood. She dabbed at it gently as she continued to try to calm Sally. "Let's just relax until we land," she said as convincingly as she could. In that instant, Sabrina realized that she was the one providing the strength they both needed. Perhaps, she considered, she had more self confidence than she gave herself credit for.

After landing and reporting their damage issues to the airline, they gladly boarded the shuttle bus that whisked them off to the casino hotel, where they hoped to have an incident-free time for the rest of their mini vacation. Upon arrival, however, they learned that there had been a mix-up in their reservations, and no room was available.

Again taking charge, Sabrina declared authoritatively, "I have the name and number of the travel agent who made these reservations for us. Please call her for confirmation."

Finally, after an aggravating forty-five minutes, the hotel admitted they had overbooked their capacity. Rather than sending the women to another hotel, they instead offered Sabrina and Sally a penthouse suite at no additional charge. Maybe they should mark the beginning of their trip as starting from this moment, Sabrina considered as they unlocked the door to their spacious accommodations overlooking all of Atlantic City.

Because Sally's neck was beginning to hurt, Sabrina recommended that they consult a doctor. A few minutes later, Sally was undergoing some basic neurological tests with the hotel's staff physician, who soon pronounced that it appeared some muscles had been strained, but there was no permanent damage. He prescribed an anti-inflammatory for the pain and a successful time in the casino as the best cure.

After the doctor left, Sabrina offered to run out to the pharmacy to pick up the prescription while Sally stood under a hot shower. "Great idea," Sally agreed, already feeling better now that she knew there was no serious injury. "We have a lot of money to make, so I better get in good shape fast."

At the pharmacy, Sabrina saw a display of Fanny Famer candies and impulsively purchased a box of French mints. When she returned to the suite, the two of them managed to scarf down half the box before deciding they would make themselves sick if they continued with their gluttony. They dressed in comfortable outfits and headed out the door to go downstairs to the casino.

At mid afternoon, the elaborately adorned gambling rooms were fairly deserted. As the women looked around, they took in the luxury that exuded from everything. Seats around the blackjack tables were comfortably padded to encourage lingering, turn of the century decorations created a feeling of opulence, and flashing lights and pleasant sounds gave the impression of plenty of payouts from the slot machines.

"Shall we stick together or split this place up and take our chances from different angles?" Sabrina asked.

"I like the slot machines," Sally answered. "How about you?"

"I think I'll try blackjack for a while. Let's meet back at the room at, say, six o'clock. We can get all gussied up and enjoy a sumptuous meal, then go to the show down the street at nine."

"Sounds like a plan. Make a million," Sally offered as she headed off to the seductively calling lights and musical tones.

Sabrina selected a table where the minimum bet was five dollars, and just watched the playing for a while. There were four people seated, all of whom seemed to be there for a good time. No one looked like a professional gambler, although

Sabrina had no idea how to tell. After a few minutes, one person lost all his chips, and blithely said that he knew when to quit. Sabrina took his seat and changed a fifty dollar bill. That would give her ten plays, enough to have fun, win a little and undoubtedly lose it all at the end, she told herself.

The dealer, a tall woman with very quick hands, greeted Sabrina with a gracious smile. The first two cards Sabrina received were a seven and a two. Nine. She tapped the table once to indicate that she wanted one more. This time she received an ace. That could count as either a one or an eleven, depending on how she wished to call it. Eleven would give her twenty, which was about as close to twenty-one as she could get. She waved her hand across her cards to indicate that she did not want any more and waited until everyone else at the table received their cards.

One player got a king and an ace, which was a blackjack. The dealer paid him one and a half times his bet, then looked at her own hand. She had a six and a four, so she dealt herself another card, which turned out to be a two. By casino regulation, the dealer was required to keep playing until she had a point count of at least sixteen, so she had to draw another card. This one was a seven, giving her a total of nineteen. The house lost to all with a score higher than nineteen, which included Sabrina. *Good start*, Sabrina thought delightedly.

For nearly an hour, Sabrina's luck went back and forth, and she left the table with fifteen dollars more than she started with. She decided to try to continue her luck by playing the slot machines but by five forty-five, had lost most of her fifteen dollar gain before she headed back to her penthouse suite.

Sally was already there, dressed and ready to go. Together, they analyzed the various outfits Sabrina had brought with her. "Which one should do you think I should wear for our first Atlantic City night?" Sabrina asked casually. "Well, it doesn't much matter. I'm not expecting to meet any fabulous men tonight."

Fifteen minutes later they were in the dining room, waiting to be seated. Sabrina looked fabulous in a dark grey pantsuit which made her already slim figure look even two sizes smaller.

FOUR

From the bar at the far end of the restaurant, he watched in stunned silence as the two women prepared to leave. He did not recognize the shorter woman, but the taller one, the one wearing the distinctive pantsuit, that one reminded him of his Sabrina, the woman he had nicknamed Sonrisa. At first, Sabrina had mistakenly thought it meant sunrise, and indeed she was his dawn, his beginning of time. But the Spanish word really meant smile, and that was what she truly was to him, his cause for smiling, his source of joy.

He had once told her that he wanted to bring her here to this city, but that was long ago when it had been a relaxed community on the Atlantic Ocean, the town where America put on its annual beauty pageant. Now it had become the epitome of the deceit of gambling interests, where the glitz of the casino area did not extend more than a block or two outside its own confines. Beyond that, neighborhoods were disintegrating and crime becoming even more rampant. How did the great

American nation allow such a thing to happen, he wondered, but Francisco knew the answer. As an economist, he knew perfectly well. Money. Greed. Apathy. His education had taught him formulas that predicted financial occurrences, but beyond that, human avarice shaped the reality of economics.

He looked again. Yes, unbelievably, he was certain that this was his beloved Sabrina, and he could clearly see that she was not wearing a wedding band. How she was here in Atlantic City at the same instant he was, he did not even try to understand. Quickly he arose, intending to rush over, pick her up and twirl her in his arms once again. In his very being, he again felt her slight body, smelled her freshly shampooed hair, heard her laughter. Then just as quickly he sat back down again, remembering that he had called her seven times in the past two days but she had never called him back, even though he left his number each time. Perhaps even now, after all these years, she could not bring herself to see or speak with him because she had so abruptly and devastatingly turned his world upside down so very, very long ago.

No, he realized, with ecstatic joy bringing a smile back to his face. She was not ignoring him. She simply did not know that he had called because she was, amazingly, here where he was. Again he arose and looked for her, but by then her table was empty. He hastily paid his bar tab and hurried into the hotel lobby. Not finding her there, he tried the casino, then returned to scour the lobby again, but she had evaporated. *Not again*, he moaned to himself. At least this time, he realized with consolation, he knew where she was living. He would keep looking for her here in Atlantic City, and if he could not find her now, he would call her in Ohio until she finally answered the phone. Indeed, if all else failed, he would just show up on her doorstep one morning.

He went back to the bar and ordered another drink, as his mind turned backward, back to the days of innocence, when love was simple and all he had to do was study hard every day and see Sabrina each night.

*   *   *

It was 1963, and he was a new graduate student in economics at this American university in Pennsylvania renowned for its progressive teaching staff. He and Sabrina had met at a mixer sponsored by the university the first weekend of the term. When he first saw this beautiful young woman, he mistook her for a graduate student because of her polished behavior and sophisticated choice of clothing. During an animated conversation about world poverty, when she told him that she was only eighteen years old, he was initially angry with himself for choosing a child to spend time with and almost walked away. However, two hours later when the mixer ended, they were still conversing over a wide range of subjects, and he decided that he definitely had not wasted his evening. Sabrina agreed to meet him the following afternoon for a soda at a restaurant near the dorm, and within a few days of meeting, they were together all the time.

"Cara Mia," he recalled saying one afternoon, "let's go to the graduate study lounge. It should be quiet and we can get a lot of work done."

"I have a chemistry quiz on Monday," Sabrina had answered. "The professor tries to make girls feel as if we aren't smart enough to study science, so I intend to get the best grade in the class."

"Poor little girl," Francisco had teased. "Why don't you give up and try something easy, maybe something artistic."

"Me, artistic?" Sabrina had burst out laughing. "For me, that would be a zillion times harder than chemistry, I assure you. My mother even tried to convince my high school principal that I shouldn't have to take art classes because my injured arm had predisposed me to never being able to utilize those muscles properly."

"But by the time you were in high school, I thought the surgeons had corrected the problem," Francisco answered, puzzlement in his voice.

"They had. But my mother assumed I could not do well in art class, and she didn't want my grades affected, so she found an excuse to get me out of art class."

Francisco laughed. "Did it work?"

"If my mother wanted something, she made it work." Sabrina's voice was both angry and proud.

"I can't wait to meet her. You make her sound like a dragon lady, but I really don't believe that."

"You're very brave. No, she isn't cruel, just very overprotective of anything that's hers. The thing is, if she thinks something is right, then that's it. No dispute, no discussion. You do it her way"

"You're here in Pittsburgh, a long way from home. She must have approved that."

"Only because, for once, her scheme didn't work. Mom wanted me to go to one of the Ivy League women's schools like Radcliffe or Wellesley. Last winter they had admission interviews over Christmas vacation, and Mom decided it would be impressive if I went alone to the interviews. She thought that would demonstrate how independent and capable I would be if they selected me to attend their school. When the interviewer told me that my parents could sit in on the appointment, I explained that I had come from Ohio alone. She didn't believe me, assuming that my parents were probably at a nearby hotel. So rather than looking like an independent young woman, I appeared to be a charlatan. Mom's great idea backfired, and I wasn't accepted at either school."

"Lucky for me," Francisco said with genuine enthusiasm, and Sabrina smiled.

When dinner time came, they walked hand-in-hand across campus to the Towers, three tall round dormitory buildings. Because they were painted a gleaming white, students had nicknamed them Ajax, Babo and Comet after the names of cleansers popular at the time. The campus cafeteria was located in the basement of the Babo Tower, and both male and female students took all their meals there.

When they arrived, they looked around for acquaintances. Seeing Pablo, a fellow Peruvian, Francisco pulled Sabrina in that direction. Pablo was seated alone, but books had been placed in front of several chairs around him, indicating that others would soon be coming back from the food line.

"Room for a couple more?" Francisco asked.

"Always," Pablo answered with a sweep of his hand. "Wendy is sitting here, and Marissa over there. There is plenty of room next to them."

Sabrina was a little wary of Pablo, who seemed to be more on the make for all the women he could find than for a solid education. Still, he was friendly and never tried to make a move on Francisco's girlfriend, so Sabrina didn't object to sitting with him.

In the line, they bumped into Betty, one of Sabrina's two roommates. Betty was an American Indian, from the Cherokee reservation in North Carolina. Attending university was Betty's first experience away from home, and Sabrina and Betty had immediately liked one another, although neither cared for their third roommate, Cheryl, who struck them both as a social snob from a well known local family.

"Hi, want to join us?" Sabrina said invitingly to Betty.

Betty glanced at Francisco, who smiled encouragingly. "Sure. I'll be right over. Thanks."

When Sabrina got back to the table, Pablo's harem, as Sabrina called it, had grown to four girls. Pablo introduced them all, then hesitated as he saw Betty approaching. His descent was pureblood Spanish and his attitude toward Peruvian Indians was condescending. However, out of courtesy to his friend's sweetheart, he maintained his friendly air and included Betty in conversations throughout the meal.

By the time everyone was into dessert, he brought up weekend plans. "Is anyone going to the Hootenanny Friday night?" he asked. His entourage immediately expressed an undying desire to do exactly that, and he was soon busy making arrangements to meet them all there. He would bring a blanket and some food, he said.

Sabrina looked at Francisco. "Judy Collins is going to be there, and I think Peter, Paul and Mary, too. It would be a good break from studying. How about it?" she asked.

"Of course, if you want to," Francisco answered happily. "I need to learn more about American culture," Anywhere Sabrina wanted to go was fine with him. "Betty, will you come with us?" he added.

"Yes, please do," Sabrina prompted, realizing that Betty would not want to be an intruder.

"Yes, thank you both very much. I would like to do that," Betty answered shyly.

"Well, it's time for us to go study some more," Francisco announced, as he helped Sabrina with her books. "We'll see everyone later."

Pablo responded, "There are many ways to study, and much to learn about here in America," as the girls around him giggled.

Back at the graduate study lounge, Sabrina and Francisco took over a table, spreading their books and papers out so no one else would come near. After a while, they had the room to themselves. Francisco moved to Sabrina's side, pulling her on to his lap. They kissed, tenderly at first, then more aggressively. Although Sabrina wanted more than kissing, her mothers' words kept buzzing in her head. *Never let a boy touch you where he shouldn't. Always maintain your dignity.* She pushed Francisco's hand away from her blouse as he tried to unbutton it. "Oh, my God," she exclaimed as she looked at her watch. "Curfew is in ten minutes. I have to get back to the dorm."

"Ooooohh!" Francisco groaned. "I don't understand this curfew business. If you are old enough to attend college, how is the school allowed to impose such a restriction on you?"

"If I had an answer to that question, I'd gladly share it with you," Sabrina answered resentfully. "It's just one of those rules we have to live with." She twitched angrily. "At least on weekends we're allowed to stay out until eleven o'clock."

"If you lived off campus, would the university watch you the same way?"

"Unmarried females under the age of twenty are not permitted to live off campus," Sabrina answered despondently.

"Ah, but male graduate students are, I imagine. I think I'll look into that. Then we would have somewhere other than graduate study lounges to go."

Sabrina's eyes sparkled with excitement. "Do you really think you could? That would be fantastic, a little place of our own. I would still have curfew, but at least we wouldn't have to study *all* the time," she added mischievously. Innocent Sabrina did not fully understand the implication of what she was saying, which Francisco understood. That was one reason he was falling in love with her. She was a shining silver dollar in a world of tarnished coins.

At the beginning of the next term, Francisco moved to an apartment, only a ten minute walk from campus. For a month and a half they studied there together and sometimes Sabrina would cook a meal. However, she continued to resist his pleas to share full love.

"Beloved, sex and love go together," Francisco tried to convince her.

Although she wanted to agree with him, she felt obliged to retort, "Francisco, if you truly love me, you will not ask this any more. I cannot make love with you. In my upbringing, sex, love and marriage go together. All three, not just two parts of it."

For the next two months, both of them became more and more frustrated. However, in April, on her nineteenth birthday, Sabrina finally decided to break with obedience to her mother's teachings and follow her own feelings instead. Although tentative at first, Sabrina soon realized that physical love was everything Francisco had promised her. "Dearest Francisco," she had breathed into his ear, "this is magical.

When we make love, the whole world goes away, and only we two are left here in this cocoon of beauty. Thank you for being so patient with me, for not going to someone else. I'm sorry I said no for so long."

Unfortunately, when talking with her mother during the obligatory weekly call home, Sabrina's joy was all too apparent, and Shirley Newsome felt alarm bells going off. The overanxious mother began a campaign to dissuade her beloved child from doing something terribly foolish, like falling in love with a foreigner. At first, Shirley tried to convince Sabrina to change to a different school, one closer to home that had a particular program in which Sabrina had once showed an interest. When that didn't work, Shirley asked a family friend to visit Sabrina and explain how difficult intercultural relationships were. When Sabrina still persisted in dating Francisco, Shirley threatened to cut off funding for college. That threat, to Shirley's astonishment, resulted in an unanticipated thrust back.

"You just go ahead and do that, Mom," Sabrina answered. "I'm nineteen, and in this state that's old enough to marry without parental consent. I'll quit school and get a job. Francisco and I will marry at the courthouse, and when he finishes next year, we'll move to Peru."

Never before had Sabrina exhibited this kind of ferocious independence, and Shirley was truly frightened. After considerable thought, she contacted the Foreign Student Office to report that one of their graduate students had seduced a freshman girl. Shirley did not believe that -- Sabrina had certainly never confessed to such a transgression -- but it was the excuse she used. Two weeks later, at the end of the term, Francisco was transferred to a different university, hundreds of miles away.

When Sabrina learned that her mother was behind Francisco's transfer, she wanted to carry through on her threat to quit school and cut herself off totally from her own family. Francisco, with a cooler head, would not hear of it.

"Beloved, disowning your family is truly the worst thing you could do. Remember that you have a father, as well as a younger sister who will always need you. Your mother is just trying to protect you. It is foolishness as you and I see it, but she has her own point of view. I'll finish school in Colorado, and you must complete your bachelor's degree here. When you are a college graduate, you will have credentials to make your own future. I can easily find a job in America. Eventually we will live our lives as we have planned, but we must do it properly."

"But why should you have to be separated from your family?" Sabrina demanded. "I can move to Peru."

"No, no, Beloved. It's not the same," Francisco answered. "I came to America to study international economics, knowing full well that such a decision might lead me to remain here for employment. Being with you in America would be entirely different from your being with me in Peru."

Eventually he convinced her that his plan would work. The following year he earned his masters degree from the school in Colorado and found a job in Peru which brought him back to the United States every three months. Over the next two years, Francisco spent as much time as possible with Sabrina whenever he was stateside. Meanwhile Sabrina drew closer to earning a dual degree in chemistry and biology, with a strong background in languages as well. At the beginning of her final undergraduate semester, she received an acceptance letter from the medical school of her choice. Their plans were beginning to coalesce.

Then, one day, Francisco recalled despondently as he sipped his drink in Atlantic City, he had received a letter from Sabrina saying that she could no longer marry him. Indeed, she had determined never to marry anyone. Furthermore, she was no longer interested in pursuing medicine, and was going to work as a secretary while she sorted out some difficult life choices. She did not elaborate on what those choices involved.

Panicked, Francisco had immediately flown back to America, but when he arrived she was no longer living at school. When he went to her parents' home and demanded to see her, her father told Francisco that he did not know where Sabrina was, and from the stricken look on his face, Francisco knew this was true. After ceaseless questions, however, they finally told Francisco that something terrible had happened to their daughter, and that she blamed her parents for it.

For a year and a half he had searched for her, but never learned where she was. Finally, he understood that his dreams with Sabrina were irrevocably shattered, and he married a girl of his family's choosing in Peru. Over the years, he fathered six children and became CEO of several international businesses. He had never returned to America since then. Not until now.

Francisco drained the last of his drink, said a brief good night to the bartender, and headed for his room, his heart both heavy and elated. His wife of thirty-two years had been taken from him by cancer a year before. Throughout her illness he had been by her bedside as she wasted away into a person he no longer recognized, but her gentle heart remained as generous as it had always been. Just before the priest pronounced last rites, she had whispered to him, "Go back and find her."

Francisco had been stunned. Somehow Angelica had known that another woman owned a piece of his being that she could never reach, and yet it had not embittered her. Such love was beyond his comprehension, and he had wept bitterly when she finally passed from this life.

Taking his wife's final word of advice, however, Francisco had now returned to Atlantic City. Although he had not known where to begin looking for Sabrina, Atlantic City was somewhere they had talked about visiting together, so it felt like a good place to launch his search.

When he called Sabrina's family home on the day he arrived, he was astonished to hear Sabrina's voice on the answering machine, rather than either of her parents'. Apparently, his Sabrina had reconnected with her family, which made him very happy. Her voice on the machine must mean that she was now living in Ohio. Finally, fate was being kind to him. Now, after so many years, he would learn why the love of his youth had disappeared, abandoning their mutual dreams and plans, with no communication, no reason.

FIVE

Taking the elevator down to the entrance level, Sabrina and Sally ambled outside to the boardwalk where they walked along in silence for a few minutes after having overindulged at the sumptuous buffet table. They enjoyed listening to the waves crashing on the shore and watching the cruise ship lights twinkling far off in the distance. After several blocks, Sally motioned to some benches. "Let's sit here and watch the crowd for a while."

For half an hour, both women talked of times they had enjoyed with their husbands, until Sabrina checked her watch. "Time to get some good seats," she announced, arising quickly as though something had spooked her. Indeed, she had suddenly felt as if there were a loving presence nearby, but looking around, she did not recognize anyone so simply dismissed it as one of those eerie feelings that happen sometimes.

As they settled into their seats, the theater filled up quickly. The comedian was excellent, and the theater thundered with laughter at the non stop antics. At intermission, the women made their way to the restroom, then came back and retook their seats. Again, Sabrina felt a presence, but could not identify it. *I'm getting superstitious or something*, she thought as she forced herself to pay attention to the jokes and not her nerves. When the show was over, Sabrina still felt uneasy and suggested that they stop somewhere for a night cap before turning in.

"I don't think so," Sally answered. "I think this body is ready for a comfortable bed and a good night's sleep."

"Okay," Sabrina agreed reluctantly. "I guess you're right. Tomorrow's another day, and we'll see what mischief we can get into then. Plus we have to confirm our return flight. Remind me and I'll do that in the morning."

Sally was immediately defensive. "I'm not flying back," she answered testily. "I'm going back by train."

Sabrina was having none of it. "If you don't fly now, you're going to have a very hard time ever getting back on an airplane again. You have to force yourself, before fear takes over. I'll admit, I'm really reluctant too, but we have to do it."

"I'm taking a train," Sally re-stated emphatically.

Sabrina didn't push. "Okay, we'll see in the morning."

When they arrived back at their hotel, they had to wait a moment for the penthouse elevator to come. "See, just look what we got out of all the problems we had coming to Atlantic City, a penthouse suite," Sabrina tried to cajole.

"The fancy accommodations are due to the travel agent's mix up, not bad weather. Good try, but it didn't work. I'm not flying back."

Sabrina laughed. "Maybe we'll go by dogsled instead."

"Very funny."

Again, just before falling asleep, Sabrina had an intimation of a presence nearby. Something about it felt good, maybe even safe, she thought somewhere in her subconscious, as she turned over and snuggled into her pillows.

The next morning both women slept until well after nine o'clock. Soon after getting up, they heard the telephone ring. It was Dr. Turner, the hotel physician.

"Good morning," he greeted cheerfully. "I'm calling as a follow up to see how you two are doing. Are you improving?" He sounded so positive that Sabrina automatically felt better.

"Physically, Sally is doing pretty well," Sabrina answered, "but she's having a hard time agreeing to get back on an airplane again."

"I'll stop by for a chat," the physician offered. "I've dealt with this before. Maybe I can help."

When Dr. Turner arrived, Sabrina went downstairs. Not long thereafter, Sally was also in the lobby, looking a little sheepish. "I guess you were right. Dr. Turner convinced me to fly home, although I don't know how he did it. He made me call to confirm our reservations, so that's done."

Sabrina beamed happily. "Fantastic," was all she said. They spent the next two days gallivanting around Atlantic City, enjoying daytime side trips and marvelous evening shows. When it was finally time to head for the airport, they gritted their teeth and took the shuttle bus. Fortunately, it was a beautiful day, with clear weather forecast all the way from Atlantic City to Cleveland.

"Time to show what we're made of," Sally announced grimly when their flight was called. When they boarded the flight, their seats were again over the wing. Sabrina took the window seat and snapped on her seatbelt. Sally sat in the center. As they taxied down the runway, the women closed their eyes and clasped hands until they were airborne.

"So far, so good," Sally said with a smile, letting go of Sabrina's hand. "Now, on the way here, I think you were telling me about this fabulous skater named Bobby. Whatever happened to him?"

Sabrina blanched, but forced her voice to stay steady. "It's not a very nice story. No one other than my parents ever knew about it."

Sally was unsure whether to ask more. "Do you want to tell me?" she asked tentatively. "I'll listen if you want to get it out of your heart."

Sabrina sighed deeply. "Perhaps it is time," which, to Sabrina, seemed both an outward statement and an inner decision. "However, there is a genuine love story to tell before I get back to Bobby."

She began so quietly that Sally could barely hear her. "When I was a freshman in high school, my father bought a store in a small town west of Cleveland," Sabrina explained. "He and my mother talked a lot about whether we should move. I was doing better socially after the operation that repaired my arm, but appropriate schooling for Anna was non-existent in the county where we lived. When Mom learned that the school district where Dad's new business was located offered a special education program for children like Anna, that clinched the decision."

"For my part, I was thrilled at the idea of moving, although I put up a bit of a fuss just for show. I realized, though, that I needed a new beginning. After the operation, some of the old crowd had opened back up and let me in, but they still remembered when I had been a little strange and there was always friction. In a new location, I figured it would be a lot easier because no one knew the old me.

"As it turned out, I was right. In high school I joined both Spanish and Russian clubs, as well as the reading club and a social group at the local YWCA. I fit in really well, dating both the football jock and the high school nerd, so everyone thought I was okay. I was even elected to Student Council a couple of times. My high school years were so much better, from a social standpoint, than junior high had been, and I was really blossoming.

"Academically, Mom made sure that I stayed at the top of my class, and when it came for the National Honor Society inductions, I was one of six students selected to induct the other forty-five kids. Mom made me keep up with all kinds of extracurricular activities, so I was a member of not only the high school orchestra but the city symphony as well. I was even a runner on the girls' track team. In other words, I was one busy little girl, and it all helped when it came time for me to apply to college.

"I wasn't accepted at the schools Mom wanted, but I was accepted exactly where I wanted to go. It was a highly regarded school in Pittsburgh, from which the acceptance rate for medical school was very good.

"I went to college with every intention of becoming a doctor, so I could do for someone else what Dr. Goodman had done for me, transform a child's life from travail into magic. My freshman year I took chemistry, math, biology, all that kind of prerequisite work. I also included both Spanish and French, which added a burden load-wise, but I really liked languages and was determined to keep them in my curriculum. There were a few battles with Mom, who thought I was compromising my scientific career, but when I managed to keep good grades, she eventually let up.

"The really big battle with Mom was about my boyfriend. His name was Francisco, and he was not from the United States. He was a graduate student from Peru." Sabrina's voice softened a little. "To this day, I still believe he was the most decent human being I've ever known -- so good-hearted, so kind, so thoughtful. He always put everyone else, especially me, ahead of his own needs." Sabrina fell silent as she reminisced inwardly for a moment. "I particularly appreciated his wonderful sense of humor. It seemed we were always laughing. He encouraged me to follow my dreams, but always to be sure they were my own dreams, not someone else's. Francisco was in a two year masters degree program in economics. I was totally, completely, head-over-heels in love with him, and I knew that my future had to be with him and no one else."

"Knowing that I would be courting disaster if I acknowledged my feelings for Francisco when Mom called every week, I tried to make it sound as if he were nothing more than a casual acquaintance. However, when she asked what I did on weekends, his name kept coming up. When she learned that Francisco was from South America, she expressed grave concern that dating a foreigner would hinder my social advancement in college. 'You won't get picked for the best sorority,' she would always say.

"When I was asked to join one of the 'good' sororities on campus, her fears were somewhat alleviated. Still, she did her best to encourage me to date other boys, saying that I shouldn't cut myself out of all the fun of being in college. As far as I was concerned, I was having the most wonderful time possible, but, of course, she didn't see it that way."

"So sweet, obedient little Sabrina was becoming her own person, huh?" Sally chuckled. "That happens in most families. How bad did it get?"

"When it became apparent that I was serious about dating only Francisco, Mom did something really rotten. She complained to the Foreign Student Office about this foreign student from Peru who was having an affair with her freshman daughter. At the end of the spring term, Francisco was suddenly notified that the State Department had decided that he needed exposure to a different philosophy of economics

-- for his own good, of course -- and he was transferred to another school, clear out in Colorado."

"Wow." Sally was horrified that a mother would do something like that, even if she thought it was for the safety of her child. "What did you do?"

"I didn't know immediately that Mom had been behind it, but when I found out, all hell broke loose. She assumed that out of sight, out of mind would work, but it didn't. I was so infuriated by her manipulation that I was ready to quit college and get married right then and there. I didn't go home for the next school break." Sabrina's face now mirrored her fury as she recalled the betrayal she had felt.

"On the other hand," she went on, "Francisco was the kind of man who believed a parent's wishes must be honored. At the time, I disagreed, but in the end it helped me see even more clearly what an upright human being he was." Softly, Sabrina blew her nose, then proceeded with her story. "After he earned his degree the following year, he returned to Peru, got a job that brought him stateside regularly, and we plowed onward, truly believing that one day we would triumph." She sighed. "But dreams don't always work out."

Here Sabrina closed her eyes and was silent for a long while. "During spring vacation of my senior year, I went home," she continued, almost whimpering. "Although by then my parents knew that Francisco and I planned to marry shortly after I graduated, we had not yet set a date and I was not wearing an engagement ring. Mom still had hopes that I would change my mind.

"It turned out that she had kept up with a few friends from where we lived when I was in elementary school and junior high. One day, one of them happened to mention remembering that I used to skate with a boy named Bobby. Now, as it happened, Bobby lived in the same town as my parents.

Mom hunted him down and, unbeknownst to me, invited him over for dinner the night I arrived home. She didn't bother to mention the invitation to me until the front doorbell rang. Although I was shocked, I couldn't stalk off and refuse to eat dinner with the family, so I made the best of it and was as courteous as I could be.

"During dinner Bobby asked me to go to the movies with him later that evening. He even said that it would make up for the one we had barely seen so many years before. Mom looked at him with surprise, but neither of us elaborated. In a way, I guess, that made us co-conspirators. Although I tried to beg off, Mom insisted that I go 'for old times' sake. To shut her up, I did.

"Bobby chose a showing at the drive-in, rather than the downtown theater. When I protested, he claimed that he had already seen the downtown movie, so again I acquiesced. *Stupid. Stupid. Stupid.*

"After buying sodas at the drive-in, he went around to his trunk, came back with a bottle of rum, wanting to spike my drink. I declined and also reminded him that he had to drive home. He just laughed and said that a little rum had never impaired him.

"Of course, my mother had neglected to inform Bobby that I was engaged to be married in a few months. When the movie started, he tried to put his hand inside my blouse and pull up my skirt, as if it was understood that we had come to the drive in for the sole purpose of having sex. When I protested, he pretended not to understand me, and chewed my lip so hard that it bled. And then when I told him I was engaged, he didn't believe me because there was no ring on my finger. Finally, I slapped him, really hard. He seemed stunned, and then he got mad, really mad." Sabrina shuddered. "At first, he just pulled back to his own side of the car and slopped more rum into his soda, then he threw the soda can away and just drank directly from the rum bottle. I was getting scared, and told him to take me home, but he wouldn't listen. He just kept gurgling down the rum. I leaned over and pulled the bottle away." Again Sabrina began trembling. "That was when the world I had known came to an end."

"My God, what happened?" Sally gasped.

"My yanking at the bottle chipped one of his teeth, and Bobby became livid. 'Fuck you,' he bellowed, and he slapped me so hard that my head felt as if it had been knocked off. I started reaching for the door handle, then I heard the locks click and I knew I was in trouble, big trouble. All the door locks were controlled from Bobby's side."

"'Who do you think you are, you little gutter snipe.' he snarled at me. 'Leading me on like a tramp. That's what you are. A tramp. I'll show you how tramps are treated,' and he doubled his fist and punched me in the stomach, so hard that I didn't think I would ever take another breath. Then he really started to hurt me – pinching my breasts as hard as he could, yanking my hair, slapping my face, just doing whatever occurred to him to cause me pain. Oh, God, I can feel that agony right now." Sabrina began visibly shaking in her seat.

"Didn't anyone see you from another car? Couldn't you call for help?" Sally was terrified for her friend, feeling as if she had been there with her on that hideous night.

Sabrina shook her head. "He had parked away from the other cars, and it was a weekday night, so there weren't very many people there anyway. No one saw. Then the bastard raped me, over and over and over, calling me a slut and a bitch and all kinds of things. Then at the end, he said with absolute conviction that he would kill Anna if I called the police on him."

"He took me back to my neighborhood and dumped me out three blocks away from my house so I would have to walk the rest of the way, as battered and bruised as I was. I slipped in the door and went straight to my room. When I was sure my parents were asleep, I went to the kitchen and got ice to put on my bruises, but I must have fainted. The next thing I knew poor Anna was screaming, then my parents were there, and I was being loaded into an ambulance. The next couple of days were a blur. The doctor tried to get me to say what had happened but I wouldn't. I had to protect my little sister." Sabrina took a deep breath. "When I finally healed, at least physically, I wrote Francisco a letter saying that I could not marry him, and then I just disappeared. For three years, I did not contact my family. I worked as a secretary or a translator or a substitute language teacher, whatever I could find. I blamed my mother entirely for what had happened, but in the end, she had won. I didn't marry Francisco."

SIX

The flight attendants gathered cups and asked passengers to put their seat backs up as they prepared for landing in Cleveland. Sally replaced Sabrina's tray table for her and patted her gently on the arm. "I know there is more to this story. Somehow you met Frank and life went on. I want to hear how after we're down," Sally encouraged.

Sabrina inclined her head compliantly, too exhausted just then to try to say any more. Closing her eyes, she somehow pulled strength back into herself. *How had she possibly said all those things*, she wondered. That poison had been buried inside her for decades. She had never gone to therapy, never told anyone, not even Frank, about the searing pain she felt inside herself every day. Why did it come out now?

Perhaps it was time, she considered. Whatever that meant. Maybe there really is a time for everything, just as Ecclesiastes had promised during her childhood Sunday school days. Sabrina scoffed at herself. It had been so long since religion had been a comfort to her. *If there is justice in this world,* she thought, *I have seldom had the luxury of seeing it. We humans are too selfish, too self-centered to allow justice to rule us.*

But, of course, that is human behavior, she reconsidered, not what we are taught through religion. *What would happen if people really did live by the teachings of their faiths?* She laughed deprecatingly to herself. *Yeah, and there is a pot of gold waiting for me at the end of the rainbow.*

The plane landed and the seat belt sign was turned off. Sabrina realized that Sally was saying something to her. "Thanks for forcing me to get back on the plane," she said. "I think I can control my fear now."

Sabrina gazed at Sally evenly and answered, "Me too. And I don't mean fear of being on an airplane. I mean fear of living."

Sally looked quizzical, and Sabrina explained. "Letting out what I just told you has been like opening a sewer and allowing fresh water to rush in where nothing but foulness has been for decades. You're right. Of course, there's more. Frank, my children, and wonderful friends like you. There is indeed so much more."

It was raining when they arrived at the parking area and Sally quickly suggested that they meet for lunch two days later. "I'll call you," she promised.

Sabrina nodded, gave her friend a bear hug, and walked to her own car. Since it was almost lunchtime, Sabrina decided to stop at Mel's Meals for lunch rather than going straight home. Mel's was a neighborhood restaurant that had proudly served local clientele since the sixties, just after Sabrina's family had moved to the area. Because Sabrina's father worked most evenings, Shirley had often brought her two daughters here to eat, and when Sabrina needed old fashioned comfort food, this was where she came.

As she walked in and shook off the rain, Mel and his wife Belle greeted her enthusiastically, while the long-time waitress looked at Sabrina with a question in her eye. Obligingly, Sabrina said, "I need the cheeseburger special today, please," as she sat down in her favorite corner booth. Everyone here knew that there were two standard lunches Sabrina ordered, a chef salad when she wanted to be good, and Mel's cheeseburger special with super greasy fries and a mound of coleslaw with a zillion grams of fat when she wanted to be very, very bad.

As soon as she sat down, Mel confronted her with a question he knew would disturb her, but needed to be asked. "How's the attic cleaning coming?" he inquired.

To his surprise, she answered cheerily. "Cleaning attics? No way. I've been off living the life of a high roller since Saturday. My friend Sally and I went to Atlantic City and we had ourselves a wonderful time. Plus, we came back almost as wealthy as we left." Then she glanced at him and added a little testily, "But to answer your question, yes, I am finally going through my attic. There's probably something up there worth a king's ransom, but right now I'm tempted to toss a match."

"You just go right on looking," Belle counseled. "You're going to find some wonderful old memories, and maybe a few things you'd rather forget. But remembering bad times isn't all that wrong a thing to do. Keeps you thinking how you can do things differently tomorrow."

Sabrina flicked her head in agreement. "Belle, you always were the essence of wisdom," she declared. "You're right. I've been reluctant to look at anything that might remind me of grief. However, life has taught me that you can't know happiness if you don't experience the other side of the coin, so once I get back to doing it, I guarantee that the attic will be totally cleaned out in two days."

"I'll bet you your next lunch that you'll still be working on it three weeks from now," Mel intoned, putting enough food to feed the town's homeless population for a week in front of Sabrina. "Here's what you need for energy."

As Sabrina was finishing lunch, Tom, her eighty-two year old next door neighbor, came in and headed straight for Sabrina's table, sitting down without asking permission to join her. Although a little younger than Sabrina's parents, Tom and his wife Martha had been surrogate stand-ins when either Sabrina or Anna needed help.

"We kept an eye on your house while you were gone," Tom said. "There was a storm Sunday night and I stopped over to see if you had any water in the basement, but it was dry, so it looks like your sump pump is working just fine."

"Thanks so much," Sabrina said appreciatively. "Do you remember when we had that thing installed? For years, Dad wanted to build a few shelves a foot or so off the floor and store things there, so if the basement flooded now and then, why worry? It wasn't until someone pointed out that the walls were starting to buckle after the lake rose that he took the problem seriously. By then, bracing up the walls cost him five times as much as installing a sump pump would have years before."

"Your Dad was a good man." Tom said with a slight admonition in his voice. "Honest and decent. Can't say that about many people anymore."

Sabrina immediately felt chastened. "Yes, he was, and thank you for saying that, Tom. I'm glad others remember him that way, too. He was an honorable man and a loyal friend."

Sabrina had not always believed that. She had felt betrayed when her dad never supported her point of view and instead allowed Shirley to be the voice of the family. After her mother died, however, her father's generous personality began to emerge, and Sabrina had been delighted to discover an intellect, a sense of humor and her father's own perspective on things that had been submerged during the years of his marriage.

"Are you headed home from here?" Tom asked.

"Briefly. Then I'm going to visit Anna. She's starting a new job."

Tom, who had observed Anna for nearly half a century, nodded. "I'll admit, my attitude toward people like Anna has done a real about face. Back in the sixties, I assumed that retarded folk couldn't do anything productive. Now look at your sister. She works everyday and pays taxes, just like the rest of us. I guess it just goes to show that educating the public – dummies like me -- can actually change someone's point of view."

"That, plus having someone like my mother next door, someone who won't let go of an idea until everyone sees it her way," Sabrina added.

"Yes, Sabrina, your Mom definitely had her ideas and wasn't shy about letting the rest of us know what they were. Even so, as much as I found her too pushy sometimes, after I had thought about what she said, I often realized she was right. She was a woman ahead of her time on a lot of things."

Sabrina nodded and sipped her iced tea, having also come to the conclusion that her mother's dominating personality had resulted in a lot of good, such as the group home where Anna now lived. Sabrina recalled all too vividly the uproar that ensued when the newly formed Association for Retarded Adults first began looking for property to house a small group of mildly retarded adults. For years, local communities stonewalled the ARA until finally, through a court order, the Association won the right to establish their first group home. From that meager beginning, the ARA had grown until it now oversaw seventy-three homes throughout the state and assisted more than one thousand adults toward moderate independence and self determination. When people gradually discovered that it cost considerably less to provide group home support than to cover the staggering cost of huge institutions, many opponents turned into supporters. Sabrina thought proudly that her mother had been instrumental in changing those attitudes. *Yes, Mother, you were a powerful personality*, Sabrina thought. *Just too powerful for me.* She smiled sadly to herself as she again caught herself conversing with her mother's shadow. It seemed that she spoke with her mother more frequently now than she had during the last few years of her mother's life. That was a shame, she knew. Such lost opportunities.

But where is the line, she wondered. How much demanding is acceptable, and when does believing you always know best become detrimental to other people? Sabrina had asked herself this question a thousand times, and over the years, she had developed an answer. You push for someone not capable of pushing for themselves, and you respect boundaries for people who have developed the skills necessary to make their own decisions, even if you strongly believe that those decisions may turn out to be wrong.

Snapping herself back to the present, Sabrina turned to Tom and asked, "How's Martha doing? You know, you two really are a special couple. I don't think I've ever heard either of you say anything negative about the other. How do you manage that?"

"We say it to each other, not about each other," Tom answered quietly. "That way we both know where we stand all the time."

"That really works?" Sabrina was amazed.

"Works as well as anything else, I reckon."

When Sabrina returned home, the message machine was

showing four new messages. They were probably all from Francisco, she thought sadly to herself. Right now, she could not handle thinking about Francisco's coming back into her life, not with everything else that had been churned up in the past few days. She deleted all the messages without listening to any of them, and headed off to visit Anna, whose group home was only eight miles away.

After pulling into the driveway, Sabrina walked to the rear of the house where she found Joanne Regan, the unflappable house mother, supervising a resident as he pulled weeds out of the vegetable garden.

"How you doing, Sabrina?" Joanne greeted. Hey, I'm glad you stopped by. Yesterday was Anna's first day at the new job, and she did right well for herself. Arianne, her job coach, was brimming with stories about how Anna listened to what she was told, helped one elderly customer get out of a tight booth, and made a highly favorable first day impression on the manager."

"Fantastic," Sabrina commented with pride. "Anna always wanted to please. What does the job entail?"

"She cleans tables over at Seventy Flavors, and she also helps with putting away the clean dishes. Anna especially likes this job because they allow her a sundae of her choice every day after work."

"Heaven help her waistline," Sabrina gasped.

"Well, that's only for the first few days," Joanne laughed, until she gets comfortable there. Arianne will work with her so she understands that it's not a good idea to eat like that all the time."

Just then Anna and her job coach arrived. When Anna saw Sabrina, she gave a little screech and ran to hug her big sister. If there was one thing Anna did well, Sabrina reflected as she was caught up in Anna's arms, it was hugs. An embrace from Anna was always heartfelt and strong and full of passion. Just pure love and appreciation. *Why couldn't more of us be like that*, Sabrina wondered. *Does simplicity of the mind somehow strengthen the spirit?*

Disengaging herself, Sabrina asked about Anna's day and was rewarded with a deluge of data. "I cleaned *all* the tables on the right side of the restuarant," Anna stated proudly. "Sam, he started there two months ago, but he just cleaned some on the left. So I did better than him, huh? Then some more people left and I cleaned two tables all over again."

"Sounds like a lot of work. How long were you there today?" Sabrina asked, love suffusing her voice.

"Just three hours today. If they like me, they're gonna let me work more next week. They're gonna like me. I know that." Anna grinned with pride.

"Of course, they're gonna like you," Sabrina responded immediately. "Who couldn't? Hey, you wanna go shopping with me?"

"Oh, boy. Yeah, sure. But first, I gotta go to my room for a minute. Oh, is it okay if I go with Sabrina, Mrs. Regan?"

"Well, you were supposed to help peel the vegetables tonight, remember? If you don't do that tonight, what could you do tomorrow to make up?"

"Tammy, her and me are good pals. I'll do her chores tomorrow if she peels potatoes for me tonight."

"Why don't you go talk with her. If she agrees, then you can go with your sister."

Anna rushed off to find Tammy, and Sabrina apologized for creating a problem.

"No, no problem at all," Joanne assured her. "Knowing they have responsibilities helps them understand that people are depending on them to carry their share, and that makes them feel important."

Again, such a simple concept, Sabrina thought. *How seldom we apply it to so called 'normal' people.*

Tammy and Anna came down together and told Mrs. Regan that they had agreed that Anna would do Tammy's chores the next night, so Anna and Sabrina immediately headed off to the mall. "Is there anything you need, Antsy?" Sabrina asked. The nickname had come from an incident years before when Anna had insisted that Sabrina buy her an ant farm she saw in a catalog.

"You know what I really want? Huh? I want a Browns sweatshirt. They're losin' a lot this year, and if I got a sweatshirt, I bet that'd help them win. Don't ya think so?"

"Absolutely. We'll stop at Wal Mart and see what we can find. Then would you like to go to Bob Evans for dinner?"

Anna's eyes sparkled as she thought about her favorite dinner, ribs in barbecue sauce. They never ate that at the group home, so whenever Sabrina came over, Anna was thrilled to go to a restaurant that served ribs, and Bob Evans was her favorite.

They pulled into the Wal Mart parking lot, which was part of an extended shopping center with a huge hobby store, an office supply store, an appliance company and several smaller businesses. As they walked into the Wal Mart, Anna spotted the wheelchair.

"Please, Sabby, push me," she pleaded.

Sabrina refused, telling Anna that she was able to walk on her own, and that was a real blessing. Anna pouted for a moment, but then was quickly back to her cheerful self. "Oooh, look," she exclaimed, pointing toward some recently installed Christmas decorations. "Is Christmas coming?"

"Well, not for a couple more months," Sabrina explained. "Some stores just start putting things up early to remind people."

They meandered slowly through the aisles, picking up little things here and there. When they found the Browns display, Anna had a hard time choosing between the orange sweatshirt with brown letters, or the brown sweatshirt with orange letters. Eventually, she chose the orange with brown, because Sabby said it looked good with her blond hair.

"Can we eat now, Sabby?" Anna asked as they walked back to the car.

With someone else, Sabrina would have teased and suggested a couple other stops first, but Anna would have been crushed. "Dinner it is," Sabrina responded heartily. As they pulled away, Anna saw a jogger with his dog running along side of him. "Look, Amigo!" she shouted.

Sabrina looked over and saw that the dog did indeed look like their childhood dog. "Do you remember how we got Amigo?" she asked Anna impulsively.

Anna shook her head.

"You'll remember when I tell you the story. We were out for one of our Sunday drives. Do you remember how we used to do that after church on Sundays?" This time Anna nodded, and then said almost spitefully, "That preacher was mean."

Sabrina was instantly sorry that she had alluded to church, recalling how their minister had told Shirley and Wayne not to bring Anna to church because other people didn't feel comfortable around her. Shirley's response had been instant and furious. "Then other people need to learn better manners," she had retorted, and Anna continued to accompany the family to services every week.

"One Sunday," Sabrina continued, "it was a beautiful fall day, like today, and we decided to take a family drive through the countryside. We were going down a dirt road, real slowly, and you saw this lump on the side of the road. You made Daddy stop, and we got out of the car to go see what it was."

"It was Amigo," Anna crowed. "But he was all beat up looking, and sad. I remember."

"Right you are, Ms. Anna. You insisted that we had to put him in the car and take him home with us. Mom was against the idea at first, but then she suddenly agreed. I'll never understand what made her change her mind like that, but into the car he went, and we took him home. Because it was Sunday, all the stores were closed in those days, so we couldn't buy any pet shampoo. Instead, we used a bar of Ivory soap and gave him a bath in the backyard. Do you remember that?"

Anna giggled. "He shook himself all over Mommy and she got mad."

"Well, not mad, really. She just ran away when he made her wet. First thing Monday morning, she had him at the vet's for a check up. The vet said he had probably been a stray for a long time, and he also told Mom that this dog would be a very good friend to the family because we had shown him kindness. That's when Mom named him Amigo. Do you remember what that means?"

"Uh, huh. You told me plenty a times. There are lots of ways people talk to each other. The words are different but they mean the same thing. Amigo means friend."

Sabrina nodded as they arrived at the restaurant and walked from the parking lot to the doors in front. As usual, there was a line, and Anna gave their name, then came back to sit down beside Sabrina on the benches. For once, the wait was not too long and they were soon seated in the non-smoking area.

"I know you probably want the ribs, but let's see what else they have tonight. How do these look to you?" Sabrina showed Anna a picture of grilled shrimp.

"Yuck, I don't like those," was Anna's response, and it was so spontaneous, Sabrina had to laugh.

"Good, then that's what I'll get, and my sister won't steal my food." They both grinned as they recalled stealing from each other's plates whenever their mother hadn't been looking.

The waitress came and took their order, and recommended that they leave room for the blueberry shortcake, which was really good that night.

While waiting for the rolls to arrive, Sabrina asked about the other people who lived at the group home with Anna, since there had been a few changes in the couple of weeks.

"I've been there the longest, so I have to be a good example. Tammy, she's real nice. Billy isn't very friendly. The others, I guess they're okay. They're pretty new. Mrs. Regan, now she's real nice. She's helping me make Christmas gifts, but I'm not gonna tell you what they are, 'cause one of them's for you." Anna grinned mischievously, delighted that she knew something her sister didn't.

The two women enjoyed a comfortable dinner together, and even ended up ordering one blueberry shortcake to share. At nine o'clock, Sabrina dropped Anna off at the group home, and without any more stops to make for herself, she drove directly back to her own house. She made herself a cup of tea and settled into the huge recliner her father had loved. That was where they had found him the day he died. He had just slipped off gently during his afternoon nap. Now, whenever Sabrina felt she needed his counsel, she would sit in this chair and talk with him.

"Dad, should I call Francisco back? Am I opening myself up for a lot more misery, or is its the right thing to do?"

She did not get an answer, but she still felt comfortable and content. She raised the foot lever and leaned back, letting the fullness of the cushions flow around her. She put her teacup on the beautiful round oak table that had been one of her parents' first acquisitions as a married couple, and she contemplated what she should do while she gradually drifted off to sleep.

Some time later, a loud ringing startled Sabrina into partial wakefulness. Automatically, she reached over to answer the telephone, without considering who might be calling so late at night. "Hello," she said sleepily.

SEVEN

"Hello, Cara Mia. Thank God you finally answered. I'm glad you're back home."

Sabrina froze, both terrified and thrilled beyond belief to hear the mellifluous sound of Francisco's voice again. Having absolutely no idea what to say, she allowed instinct to take over for her.

"Hello, Francisco," she replied, trying to keep the breathless agitation she felt out of her voice. "I'm doing very well. How did you find me? How are you and your family?" She deliberately added the inquiry about his family to put their conversation on a proper setting. "Where are you?" She almost added *when can I see you*, but bit her tongue in time. Then realizing that he had said he was glad she was back home, she asked, "How did you know I was away from home?"

"So many questions." He was laughing, that bubbling

sound from deep inside his being that Sabrina had yearned to hear for so long. "Beloved, I am ecstatically wonderful, now that I am talking with you again." The joy in Francisco's voice resonated across the telephone line and straight into Sabrina's heart. "Actually, I am here in the United States for a while. . ."

"You're here?" she interrupted. "Where? Are you anywhere near Cleveland?"

"Actually, I'm in Atlantic City. I saw you here. You were with a woman friend, in a restaurant. I started to come over to your table, but by the time I arrived, you were gone. I looked all over the hotel, and even the casino, but I couldn't find you anywhere. Oh, my beloved, I was *so* disappointed. I wanted so much to come and hold you and tell you how much I still love you."

Now the haunting feelings Sabrina had felt in Atlantic City began to make sense to her. "I felt a presence on several occasions," she said, "but when I looked around, I didn't recognize anyone."

"You see, my dearest, we still communicate, with neither sight nor touch. It has always been that way. It always will be. Our love is something very special, something beyond comprehension."

Sabrina did not answer. What could she say? How could

she explain what had happened all those years ago? Instead, she began talking about why she was back living in Ohio. "My husband Frank died about five years ago. I felt a need to come back here to sort out what had happened in my life so I could try to repair some major errors I made with my children."

"Oh, Sabrina, I am sorry that you lost your husband. I, too, lost my wife, Angelica. She died of cancer a year ago."

Sabrina's heart throbbed in sympathy. She had held the hands of friends in hospices as they spent their final days enduring the ravages of cancer. She knew the agony for both the patient and for those who loved them. "Oh, Francisco, I am so sorry. Cancer. Such a cruel thief." Her voice reflected the affinity she felt for his loss.

"Sabrina, we both had separate lives for so long, and now perhaps it is right that we should find each other again. It is time."

Sabrina did not know what to say, how to explain. She remained silent for a long, long time.

Understanding her quietness, Francisco spoke for her. "Sabrina, I know what happened," he said gently. "Your parents told me about the man named Bobby. They told me you had disappeared and that no one could find you. I refused to believe them and I searched for more than a year. Finally, however, I understood that you did not want to be found. It was so hard, but I realized that I had to honor the choice you made, even though I had not been allowed to be part of it."

Sabrina was aghast. She had no idea that Francisco had ever known about Bobby. "*What* did my parents tell you?" she demanded.

"They told me the truth, Beloved, although they would not tell me who he was. They were afraid I would find him and do him harm. Of course, they were right. I would have killed him."

"They promised me they would never tell anyone," Sabrina shouted, then calmed herself. "That evil creature threatened Anna if I called the police, and I had to protect her." By now Sabrina was sobbing, knowing deep within herself that Francisco would somehow comfort her.

"Dearest Sabrina, that was yesterday. Let it remain there." Francisco's voice softened. "Please, when may I come to see you? We will talk, and we will understand one another just as we always did."

After a moment, Sabrina answered softly. "Yes." It was all she was able to say.

"I'll call you just as soon as I've made reservations." Then he added, "You are still the foundation of my being, Cara Mia. You always have been. You always will be."

Still sobbing, Sabrina managed to say, "Francisco, I am so sorry. So very, very sorry. I wish we could turn back time and be carefree and happy again."

"No, my love. Life has taken us on its path. We cannot change what is past. But we can always control how we deal with it, and what we learn from it. Life, my love, is a balancing act, offsetting harsh occurrences with happy moments. Those moments of happiness allow us to endure the times of tribulation."

"Oh, Francisco, you were always so wise, so compassionate. Thank you. I will be counting the tenths of each second until I see you. Let me know as soon as you can."

"Good night, Beloved. Rest well. I'll call you tomorrow."

"Good night, Francisco. I love you." Sabrina was startled at how those words slipped right past her effort to stop them.

Gently, she replaced the receiver and settled back into her father's chair. "Is this right, Dad?" she asked. "Miraculously, we are both single. But are we the same? Will we ever be able to go back to where we were?"

In the back of her mind, she heard her father's wise voice. Since her mother had died, Sabrina had begun to appreciate how much her father had always wanted only the best for her, even though he did not always provide it. *My child*, the voice in her head said, *nothing is ever the same as it once was. But that does not mean it is not worth pursuing. Follow your heart. Only that will lead you right.*

Slowly she made her way out of her father's chair and back to her bedroom. She switched on the light, opened the heating vent, and crawled into the bed of her childhood. Happily, she melted into the comfort of flannel sheets on a cool night and slept like an infant.

In the morning, not wanting to formally acknowledge that it was time to get things done, she stayed in her nightgown and padded down the hall to the kitchen, where she rummaged around in the refrigerator until she found her English muffins. Slicing one in half, she dropped both pieces into the toaster, then chose lemon tea from her assortment in the cupboard and turned on the electric kettle. On the kitchen table was a basket of fruit, and she selected an apple, which was a habit from the years of her marriage to Frank. Frank had loved fruit, and always wanted to see it on the kitchen table each morning. Sabrina maintained this habit in his memory.

When the English muffins popped up, Sabrina spread them with cream cheese, then sat down at the kitchen table with a pencil and paper to begin planning her day. She determinedly did not allow herself to think about last night's phone call, for fear that daylight would prove it had only been a dream.

First, she would pay her growing stack of bills. That chore took almost an hour and left her feeling grumpy. Next on the list was a reminder to call Anna's group home about an upcoming fund drive which she had promised to coordinate. That one she was happy to do, since she enjoyed chairing committees and seeing money come in for good causes, as she had often done when her children were youngsters. Then a couple of calls to make appointments for her hair coloring and an annual physical, and finally it was time to go back up to the attic. By now it was almost ten thirty, far later than she had planned on for getting started on the real work of the day.

Today she intended to tackle some of the boxes with her mother's handwriting on it. *Probably more old magazines*, Sabrina hoped. *Easy to get rid of.* As Sabrina struggled with the tape holding the boxes securely closed, she gasped when she finally got the top off. Recognizing her own handwriting on envelopes that had long since turned yellow, Sabrina realized she had found letters she had written to her parents decades before. With trepidation, she organized the letters by date and began to peruse them, beginning with the oldest. How well she remembered the amount of persuasion Frank had had to exert before she finally agreed to mail that one, the letter that had begun her reintegration into her family. Oh, how conflicted she had been about sending it.

Slowly, she began to read, noticing immediately that there

was no *Dear,* no indication of warmth or familiarity. It was as if she had been writing to a magazine company to change her subscription date. Well, that was, indeed, pretty much how she had felt at the time.

Mother and Dad, it had begun . . .

Although I no longer choose to have a relationship with either of you, that does not negate my feelings for Anna. She will always be my sister, and I fully accept responsibility for her when the two of you are gone. Because of her diminished capacity to understand or perhaps even remember, I believe it is now necessary for me to re-establish ongoing contact with her.

In order to do that, regretfully, I must go through you. As you can see from the return address, I am living in Indiana, only seven hours away from Anna. I would like to see her on the first weekend of June. If this is convenient, please write back to confirm that it will be satisfactory for me to pick her up on Saturday morning at 10:00 AM.

And it had been signed Sabrina, without even a *sincerely,* certainly not a *love*.

Three days later her telephone had rung, with her father on the other end, telling her that he and Mom were so grateful she had finally contacted them. He said he had found her telephone number through directory assistance, which

Sabrina knew was not true because she had insisted on having an unlisted number when she fled Ohio. For years she had been frightened of being found, not only by her parents but even more terrifyingly, by Bobby. Many a night she had awakened, drenched in a cold sweat, as she relived yet again the nightmare of his smirk, his hands all over her body, his stinking breath.

Undoubtedly, she decided, her father had hired a private detective to track her down, once he had her address. Well, at least for three years she had successfully avoided being found, and she was proud of that. As she listened to her father's voice, over and over she heard the word love, and finally her mother came on the line. Shirley told her daughter that she understood how deep her feelings of betrayal must be, and could they please talk about it? Her mother even said that she had gone to a therapist, where she learned how dominating she appeared to her family. Throughout it all, Sabrina barely acknowledged hearing anything, but she did say that she would pick Anna up on the designated Saturday morning. After hanging up, she had desperately needed to talk with someone, and she automatically turned to the one person she had begun to trust.

Reaching Frank in Chicago, she told him briefly about the conversation with her parents. Hearing the desperation in her voice, Frank had driven to Indiana immediately to be with her.

By the time he arrived, Sabrina had begun to unthaw from her long frozen feelings toward her parents, and Frank helped her maintain sanity through one of the most difficult afternoons of her life. *Without him that day, what would have happened to her*, she wondered.

Frank. Truly the man who had saved her overflowing life. Sabrina sat on the floor in the attic and leaned back against the ancient trunk, remembering how he had gradually managed to break down the barricades she had so carefully constructed around herself before she met him.

*   *   *

When Sabrina decided to flee her parents' home, she had literally thrown a dart at a map. It landed in a little town southwest of Indianapolis called Vincennes. Sabrina told herself that the landing of the dart must have special significance, since one of her favorite childhood books had been Alice of Old Vincennes, a story of a girl who had suffered many hardships during the days of early American settlement.

Thanks to working during the last two years of college, Sabrina had a small amount of savings accumulated. Therefore, her first couple of weeks of self exile were spent locating a decent apartment and furnishing it exactly as she wanted. She haunted antique shops and yard sales, and defined her living conditions exactly as she wanted for the first time in her life. Rather than the café curtains that her mother had selected for her bedroom when she was in high school, Sabrina now chose heavy full length draperies. Her furniture was dark pecan, not the light oak of her childhood. The kitchen table was wooden, which her mother had always frowned upon, and she deliberately bought an electric can opener, which her mother had always thought frivolous. In honor of Francisco, she put out one of the few mementos she had retained from their relationship, a hand carved wooden Peruvian bowl that he had once given her for no particular reason. *Just because I thought you would like it*, he had said.

Being proficient in languages, she was able to find work as a substitute teacher and tutor within the public school system, despite being one semester short of a college degree. Little by little her reputation grew until she was also being asked to do some work for private businesses with overseas contacts. Eventually she was working full time for a translating company, and one day her supervisor asked if she could assist someone at an international business conference in New York City. This person needed a translator who was fluent in French, Spanish and Russian, and the usual interpreter was off on another job.

At first she had refused, fearing childhood memories of family trips to New York. However, the supervisor had insisted, and finally she acquiesced. At O'Hare Airport in Chicago, she met the man for whom she was to translate in the first class lounge. He wanted to go over some basic data to be sure she understood the nature of his business and the matters he would be discussing at the trade show. His name was Frank Olensky, and he was one of five children born to Russian immigrants. Two of his younger brothers also participated in the import business, but Frank selected the merchandise and oversaw the wholesaling to retail stores, while his brothers were involved in the accounting and legal aspects of the business.

At first sight, Sabrina instinctively found him frightening. Although he was courteous, he was very tall, nearly six feet five inches, and very, very blonde. His eyes were ice blue. Sabrina's first impression was that Mr. Olensky was a hired assassin.

He seemed to sense her apprehension, probably because it was a typical reaction to his size and bearing. He sat at the far end of the table in an effort to avoid making her feel crowded. When it came time to board the plane, he made an excuse to sit in the aisle seat which happened to be open across from her. They continued to converse, and gradually Sabrina's feelings of intimidation began to lessen.

At the hotel in New York, their rooms were on separate floors. Sabrina took the elevator to her room on the eighth floor, double locked her door and sank onto her bed, now almost shaking from memories of childhood trips she had taken to this city in the past with her parents and Anna. At least this was a different hotel from where she had stayed way back then. She closed her eyes and forced her mind to shut out everything, only allowing herself to listen to the New York traffic in the streets below.

Finally she arose, and after a soothing soak in the tub, Sabrina dressed for dinner. The hotel dining room was elegant, and she did not want to embarrass the man for whom she was working, so she put on her trim black sheath and carefully applied a little makeup. At the last moment, she dabbed a bit more red on her cheeks. Satisfied, she gathered her pocketbook and door key, and straightened her shoulders. "This is business, not a trip from childhood," she told herself severely. "Now act like an adult and do not let Mr. Olensky know that there are any ghosts in your closet."

With that, she had closed the door behind her confidently, and marched to the elevator. There were mirrors by the elevator, probably for people to look at themselves so they did not realize how long they were waiting for the elevator, Sabrina thought. She was startled to see a full length reflection of a beautiful woman. She hastily looked around, but she was alone. She straightened her spine and smiled at herself. "Hey, you're not so bad," she said to the mirror.

Mr. Olensky was waiting in the dining room, and he arose to pull out Sabrina's chair as she approached. He remarked briefly on how nice she looked, then immediately turned to the menu. After a moment's perusal, he recommended the shrimp scampi, which he said was excellent at this hotel.

Not liking seafood at that time, Sabrina said that she would prefer the Beef Wellington, to which Mr. Olensky responded with a chuckle and a remark about liking a woman who knows what she wants. He turned to the waiter and ordered Beef Wellington for the lady and the scampi for himself.

During dinner, they talked about the conference the next day and which dealers he particularly wanted to work with. He warned her about various tricks he had seen played over the years, especially with nuances of words, and told her to be very exact in her translation. Sabrina listened carefully and was impressed both with Mr. Olensky's knowledge and his wisdom. She gained the impression that he was fairly well versed in several languages himself, but did not want his business associates to know. When the meal ended, she was vaguely disappointed that the evening had to come to a close. By then he had insisted that she call him Frank, and she finally felt comfortable doing so.

Back in her room, she carefully hung her clothes in the closet, then, saying a small prayer to an unknown source, since her faith in the God of her childhood was long gone, she asked that tomorrow would go well and that she would translate effectively for her temporary employer.

Why, she wondered, had she been so reluctant to call him Frank, when he was obviously only a few years older than herself? She thought for a moment and realized that he did not wear a wedding band, and had said nothing about a wife or children. Actually, he had said very little of a personal nature. Other people she had translated for had seemed more open. *Well, everyone is different*, she told herself. She switched on the television and fell asleep with the lights on.

She awoke with a stab of fear in her heart. What had she heard? She moved her eyes, but not her head. Gradually, as she focused her mind on where she was, she realized that what she heard was the buzzing of static. Smiling to herself at her jumpiness, she switched the TV off, rolled over and went back to sleep.

The next time she heard something, it was her wake up call. She groaned, feeling that she had been awakened from an important dream, and picked up the phone. However, it was Frank, not the hotel switchboard.

"I'm so sorry to call this early. I had a message when I got back to my room last night, and I have to clear up a couple of things this morning. I won't be able to meet you for breakfast, so I'll see you near the French booths at ten o'clock."

"The French booths. Of course. I'll see you there," she had answered.

Sabrina now had more time in her morning, and wondered what to do with it. She looked at her clock and saw that it now was 7:30 AM, just as the phone rang again. This time it was her wake up call. She decided to take a quick walk to clear her mind for the day ahead. She put on the business suit she would wear during the day, but a comfortable pair of shoes. *This must look spectacular*, she thought wryly to herself, *a dressy outfit and flat shoes.*

As she exited the revolving doors her coat got caught, and the man behind her helped her to extract herself. He introduced himself as one of the exporters at the Import-Export Show being conducted at the hotel. He immediately insisted on walking with her, saying suavely that he could not allow a beautiful woman to stroll unaccompanied in downtown New York City. He was so totally impressed with himself that Sabrina could not get a word in for more than two blocks. When he finally deigned to ask her why she was staying at the hotel, she explained that she was there as an interpreter for an importer. Prior to that, the man had been bragging about how he knew exactly how to best any entrepreneur. Now, he was shocked to learn that he had been giving away secrets to a potential adversary. Immediately, he threatened his walking companion with exposure to her professional association if she in any way revealed what she had heard from him.

By this time Sabrina was incensed. First, the lout had forced his presence on her. Then he had blathered all his ideas with absolutely no encouragement from her. Now he was threatening her as if she had done something unethical.

"Monsieur," she said, now speaking in very formal French, "I have not asked for your company. I have not asked for your ideas. I have not asked for your threats. If my employer has any dealings with you today, I will translate exactly what is said, as I always do. I expect you will represent your interests to your best advantage, just as I will do for my employer."

With that, she turned on her heel and marched off in the opposite direction. Well, so much for a pleasant stroll along New York City streets, she decided. Actually, there probably was no such thing as a pleasant stroll in New York City, with all the people jamming against one another and hurrying to get wherever they were going. She walked the three blocks back to the hotel and just barely dodged out of the way of a taxi as she crossed the street. It was 9:35 AM when she finally got back to her room. Just as she put her key in the lock, the door opened and a heavy set man in a dark suit confronted her.

"Is this your room, Madam?" he demanded.

"I will ask the questions," Sabrina retorted, staying in the hallway. "Why are you coming out of my room? How did you enter, and with whose permission?"

The man laughed mirthlessly. "I work for security at this hotel, Madam. The maid called to say that it appeared your room had been ransacked. I came to investigate."

"What?" Sabrina was stunned. "Why? I have nothing of value. I am an interpreter for the Import-Export trade show."

"Please look through your belongings, and tell me if anything is missing," he commanded highhandedly as they entered her room. Sabrina looked with despair at her dumped suitcase and emptied drawers. After reviewing the chaos, she told the man that a ring and a bracelet were missing, as well as her housekeys. "Is robbery a typical problem in this hotel," she asked angrily.

"No, Ma'am. Usually it occurs only when someone has something of great value and doesn't bother to give it to the front desk for placement in the safe."

"That is certainly not the case here," she spat out angrily.

The detective looked at her curiously, then suggested, "Nothing that might be of interest to an exporter?"

"Like what, for instance?" Sabrina demanded. *What was it with New York City? A Frenchman threatens her because he can't keep his mouth shut, and a detective acts as if she is secreting valuables overseas.* Good God, all she was doing was filling in for someone who couldn't make an interpreting job.

Finally, the detective left. Sabrina told the maid not to touch anything, and she hastily changed her shoes. By the time she got to the French booth, it was 10:15 AM, and Frank was looking annoyed. Before he had a chance to say anything, she asked if they could speak over in the corner and she walked away from him so he had no choice but to follow her. Briefly, she explained about the Frenchman, whom she pointed out across the room, and then described her interaction with the detective at her room. Frank looked amazed, then furious.

"Monsieur La Pelle," Frank said. "I have dealt with him before. Don't let him bother you. There are several other French exporters, and I will confine my business to them. LaPelle has nothing that I can't get elsewhere, and he has always been annoying, with his arrogance. Now tell me again, what is it that you are missing from your room? I will replace everything. This is my fault, and I am so very sorry."

Having expected Frank to be angry that she had potentially hindered his business dealings, Sabrina was astonished at this response. She assured him that nothing of significant value was gone, and that the hotel detective had told her the hotel's insurance would cover her loss.

"No, I insist that we will go to a jeweler and replace what was stolen. No argument." Frank said this with such authority that Sabrina did not disagree further.

They spent the day finalizing purchases, and by late afternoon Frank was extremely pleased with his success. Sabrina had indeed caught a couple of nuances and her clarifications had saved Frank several thousand dollars. By five o'clock, they were both exhausted.

"I have a proposal," Frank recommended. "Tomorrow we need to do a little more bargaining, and then I will be finished with all this for another six months. Tonight, let's have dinner at a fabulous Turkish restaurant I know of over on Houston Street, and tomorrow afternoon we will go shopping for your jewelry."

The way he said it was so irresistible that Sabrina could not say no. The Turkish dinner was delightful, and by the end of the evening, Sabrina was looking forward to replacement shopping with Frank the next morning.

EIGHT

The jewelry shopping became unnecessary, however. By the following morning, the Chief of Security had called to inform Sabrina that her jewelry and keys had been recovered, and the person responsible apprehended. It turned out that the perpetrator was a cat burglar, recently released from New York's infamous prison, Rikers Island. He had randomly selected Sabrina's room, as well as the rooms of four other guests at the hotel. The hotel apologized profusely, and offered Sabrina a complimentary room the next time she was in New York City. Sabrina replied tartly that she did not expect she would be returning to either this city or this hotel very soon.

On the plane back, Frank sat next to Sabrina, rather than across the aisle, and this time they chatted comfortably about personal matters. Sabrina learned that Frank was very active in the Russian Orthodox Church, taught swimming at the YMCA to underprivileged youth, and loved horseback riding. Both of his parents were still living, and his family was close knit.

His father was a retired ophthalmologist who had brought the family to the United States after World War I to escape the communists. Frank had a younger sister who was a student a drama school in Chicago, two brothers who were not involved in the import business at all, and two others who were. Frank had never married, although most of his siblings had.

"I'm the eldest son, so I had to make the family name famous in the business world," Frank joked. "I was expected to become a wealthy entrepreneur, like any good American." Behind the raillery, however, Sabrina thought she heard a sadness.

Sabrina told Frank that she was a few credits short of receiving her undergraduate degree, but did not mention her scientific background or the fact that she had been accepted at a prestigious medical school. When Frank asked if she had a boyfriend, she answered, perhaps too quickly, "Not right now."

When they left the plane at O'Hare, Frank thanked her for her expertise. "There's no way I would have been so successful without your able guidance," he told her. "I have to go to New York every six months, and I look forward to having you help me again."

Sabrina nodded non-commitally, said some parting words that she hoped were appropriate, and headed off for her train to Vincennes. Although she had enjoyed the change for a few days, she was now glad to be back where she felt safe. Being with a man for three full days and evenings without respite had exhausted her and she felt unsettled, even though the assignment itself had not been particularly difficult.

A few days later her supervisor called her, this time with an assignment in Chicago. "Same fellow," Neal said. "He has someone coming in from some African country where they speak French, and he needs a translator."

This time, Sabrina refused the offer, saying that she thought she had caught a cold and could not travel. The following week Neal called yet again, saying that Mr. Olensky was coming through Vincennes the following Tuesday and wanted to meet with Sabrina to discuss some upcoming jobs. However, when Neal saw that Sabrina looked somewhat uncomfortable, he immediately became protective of his employee.

"What's with this guy? Is he hitting on you or something? If that's it, I'll tell him to buzz off. He uses our company instead of one in Chicago because he's an old classmate of mine, but I won't put up with clients bothering my employees."

"No, no, that's not it," Sabrina replied hastily. "He's nice. Actually, he thought I caught a couple of trick phrases that saved him some headaches, and I guess he's grateful. I'll be glad to spend a few minutes with him when he comes," she responded reluctantly to her boss.

*   *   *

Now sitting on the attic floor, Sabrina acknowledged that Frank's visit to Vincennes had been the beginning of her return to life. Somehow that afternoon, Frank had convinced her to accompany him to dinner, and afterwards they sat talking in the coffee shop until the owner shooed them out at midnight. The next day they drove to Indianapolis. Frank wanted to see how many stores were carrying his products, and was as delighted as a child when he found many items that he had imported in shops all over town. Sabrina thought he was pulling her leg a little. *Wouldn't he know who was ordering from his company,* she wondered. But it was fun to see him so tickled with his ability to provide 'foreign goods' to the heartland of America.

On the way home, Frank had pulled off to the side of the road. "Today is my birthday," he announced. "Does the birthday boy get a kiss?" Without waiting for a reply, he pulled her close and secured his present. To her surprise, Sabrina was not horrified, although she did feel a stab in her stomach that warned of trouble if anything more occurred, but nothing did.

The next time Frank invited Sabrina to Chicago, she went, clearly understanding that this was a personal invitation. After a day at the stock exchange, the Sears Tower, and a boat ride down the Chicago River, Frank took Sabrina to his parents' house for dinner and to meet the family.

The whole tribe was there. At first, Sabrina had been overwhelmed, but his raucous family had been so accepting and warm that her reticence quickly faded. Two of the brothers looked like twins, even though they weren't. Sabrina kept getting them mixed up, and they played on her confusion, which amused everyone, including Sabrina herself. Sabrina found herself not only joining in on the camaraderie, but actually enjoying it. In truth, she later admitted to herself, it made her miss her own family life. She had not told Frank that she had disowned her parents, but he seemed to intuitively know that something was askew when she talked only of Anna, never her parents. Then one day, he had come right out and confronted her. "Sabrina, why are you estranged from your parents? What happened?" Although his concern was genuine, she would not give him an answer.

"It's something I can't talk about," she responded, tears welling up in her eyes. "There's no hope for reconciliation."

"Nonsense," Frank exploded. "Of course there's hope. There's always hope. It all depends on how stubborn people want to be."

Sabrina was flabbergasted by his response, and became vehemently defensive. "You don't know what you're talking about," she shouted. "Don't try to tell me how to deal with my family. You just don't know."

"What I do know," he remonstrated more gently, "is that you are hurting something awful. I'd like to pluck that hurt right out of your life, if I could. But I can't. So I'll be here whenever you want to talk about it."

"That will be never," she asserted. When she returned toVincennes after that visit, she vowed never to go back to Chicago again.

Eventually, however, she had gone back to Chicago, and, after considerable soul searching, Sabrina discussed her hurt with Frank. By this time, to her amazement, she was finally allowing herself to trust another man, at least partially. However, her revelations remained limited to the fact that she was estranged from her parents, but not her sister Anna. Sabrina never explained the true reason for the estrangement, and instead blamed the problems on her mother's dominating personality.

With Frank's gentle encouragement, Sabrina finally acknowledged that she was being stubborn as well as selfish. Anna, she conceded, was the one who was suffering the most. Frank asked what would become of Anna when her parents died, and he pointed out that Anna had done nothing to deserve Sabrina's desertion. After several days of discussion, Sabrina had finally crafted this letter to her parents, and after several more days, she had sealed it and finally dropped it into the mailbox.

Now here it was, in her hands again, bringing back so many disparate thoughts and recollections. Of Frank's gentle encouragement until she finally relented and allowed herself to let her parents back into her life. Of Anna's unrestrained joy when her big sister pulled into the driveway that Saturday morning. Of Frank's patience as she began to peel away the layers of hurt and anger and bitterness and hatred and God knew how many other feelings until she was down to her own core, from which she could gradually embark on a journey to rebuild. Of Frank's understanding when they finally lay side by side in bed, and she still pulled away and said no.

One time Sabrina told Frank about her deformed arm and the miraculous surgery. She analyzed her false friends in junior high, her religious doubts, her despair about ever being free of her mother's domination. Eventually, she even told Frank about her college sweetheart, but she never, ever told him about the rape. That horror was something she still could not put into words at that point in her life.

NINE

Sabrina glanced at the portable clock she had brought to the attic with her. It was almost eleven o'clock, and she hurried downstairs to change for lunch. By noon, she was at the Big Boy on Old Route 10, waiting for Sally to drive up in her flashy red Miata. A few minutes later, Sally spun into a parking space, tires screeching.

"Hey, pal," one of these days the cops are going to get you," Sabrina bantered.

"Right after they pull you over for snail pacing," came Sally's impertinent reply. "Now listen. I have fantastic news for you, something you'll really like."

Sabrina cocked her head and raised an eyebrow.

"The Madrid Madrigals are performing at the community college next week," Sally disclosed. "I have a friend at the box office. Shall I get tickets?"

This troupe of Spanish folk dancers and flamenco artists were an enduring favorite of Sabrina's, and her answer was spontaneous. "And how!" she hooted. Then, realizing that Francisco would be there next week, she added "Which day is it?"

"Thursday evening, seven o'clock."

"Could you get three tickets?" Sabrina asked, smiling broadly.

"Who's visiting?" Sally asked.

"Francisco."

"*What*?" Sally couldn't believe her ears. "*The* Francisco?"

"*The* Francisco." Sabrina was grinning so joyously that Sally couldn't help but be infected by her happiness, although she was instantly suspicious of this sudden reappearance.

"How did that happen?" Sally demanded as she glanced at the menu.

"You're not going to believe this. He was actually in Atlantic City last week. He even saw us there."

"Then why didn't he rush over to reclaim his long lost love?" Sally was incredulous.

"He tried. He spotted us as we were about to leave the

buffet the first night we were there, but we left before he could get over to our table," Sabrina explained. "He looked all through the hotel and the casino, but by then we were strolling down the boardwalk, so he never found us. Since he didn't know my married name, he couldn't leave a message at the desk for me.

Sally stared at her friend, whose babbling wasn't convincing her. "He could have left a note with the front desk clerk, along with your description and a twenty dollar bribe. The clerk would have gotten the message to you," Sally stated emphatically. "There were lots of ways he could have contacted you there in Atlantic City, if he was so concerned about your whereabouts."

Sabrina took a deep breath and tried again. "By then, he knew that I was living back at my parents' home in Ohio. He had called here and heard my voice on the answering machine, so he realized that he could find me here if not in Atlantic City. Last night, Sally, it felt like a jigsaw puzzle finally fitting together perfectly. Actually, it felt like . . . oh I don't know, like . . . it just felt right," Sabrina finally blurted out.

Sally gave an enormous sigh, then answered slowly. "So what does that mean, he's coming to see you? To pick up where he left off four decades ago? Or maybe just to say hi and disappear for another four decades. Is he still married, looking for a fling? What's going on here?"

"That's not fair," Sabrina retorted sharply. "I'm the one who disappeared, not Francisco. He has several adult children, and his wife died last year of cancer. There's nothing underhanded going on."

"Maybe that's what you see right now." Sally was still not convinced that this sudden contact was in her friend's best interests. "How do you really know?"

"Look, he spent a year looking for me in the sixties." Sabrina was becoming very defensive. "By some miracle, now we are back in touch. Sally, I have to see where this leads."

"Are you sure you want to do this?" Sally asked kindly. "Can you really risk opening those old, old wounds? Maybe it's better to let the past stay in the past."

"I don't know," Sabrina conceded, her eyes beginning to glisten. "But in my soul, I feel I have to straighten out the jagged path I left behind me. I don't know what is really right, but it feels to me as if this is."

"Did you talk at all about your children? Or Frank? What does he know about who you have become?"

"Not much yet," Sabrina admitted. "But I will tell him everything. And Sally, I've withheld so much about my life from you. I'm sorry. Maybe like the story of the rape, it's time for me to confront some other demons as well." As they ate a slow lunch, Sabrina told a tale of maternal bliss turned into anger, bitterness and sorrow.

"After Frank and I married, we chose not to have children for a while. Truthfully, we didn't want interference with the wonderful life we were enjoying which involved lots of international travel and not much personal responsibility. At that time, my main function was to help Frank's business grow, and I loved doing it. As well as going to New York twice a year for trade shows, we began to travel overseas to manufacturing plants, and Frank met a lot of businessmen with whom he would later become engaged as an international trade negotiator. I continued to function as his interpreter, and after the work part of the trip was over, we would go on side excursions, skiing or on a Mediterranean cruise or something. It was an idyllic life for the first few years.

"Finally, however, when we decided to start a family, I became pregnant quickly. Our oldest daughter, Karenna, was born when I was 31. Oh, Sally, you should have seen Frank with her that first day in the hospital." Sabrina's eyes shone at the memory. "Frank had her future planned right through graduate school before she was six hours old. It was wonderful to see how much he loved her, and I was sure my life had become perfect.

"As new parents, we fumbled along, making and correcting mistakes, until Frank and I had our first severe falling out over something I don't even remember now. Then my mother jumped right back into trying to run my life, completely forgetting the lessons I thought she had learned about how her domination caused problems that spiraled out of even her control. She insisted that she was protecting the best interests of her grandchild only because, in her words, 'Frank and I weren't doing so ourselves'. Her intentions were good, as always, but her interference caused even more strife between Frank and me. This time, however, since he was the one usually being maligned, Frank understood how I had felt for so long, and even he finally began to disengage from contact with her.

"Two and a half years after Karenna's arrival, our son Paul entered our lives, and again Frank was ecstatic beyond belief. This was his son, the one who would inherit his business and expand it into an international conglomerate. Just as with Karenna, Frank planned out Paul's trajectory, even reserving a spot in a prestigious kindergarten program for him before his first birthday.

"After Paul's birth, I suffered two miscarriages. To my shock, Frank blamed me, saying that I wasn't taking proper care of myself. This time, our worlds really began to drift apart. He insisted that I should sit on the sundeck with a book in my hand all day long. 'Let the maid take care of the kids and do the housework', he would yell, and then he would stomp away when I tried to explain that I couldn't just vegetate all the time.

"At the same time, the doctor was telling me that my miscarriages were probably related to my age. He instructed me in no uncertain terms to be content with the family I already had, and that created a quandary for me. Should I obey my doctor or my husband, who wanted at least one more child? I had to figure out what I really wanted for myself, but it turned out that wasn't hard. I knew I wanted another child, as did Frank, so we ignored the doctor.

"When I was in my late thirties, Sarah came to us. She was my baby, always and forever. Even," here Sabrina hesitated for a moment, and her voice quavered, "even now that she is no longer with me.

"Can you tell me what happened to Sarah?" Sally asked, knowing that this was a pain so deeply buried that Sabrina had never pulled it out to examine it.

Sabrina shook her head mournfully, paused for a moment, then went on with her story. "I loved being a mother, and I put my whole heart into it. I took the three of them with me whenever I went shopping, threw huge birthday parties for them, invited all the neighborhood kids to my house all the time, dispensed wisdom like a guru sitting on a mountaintop. Overall, I became totally infatuated with how great a mom

I was. Of course, with three kids, I no longer participated in Frank's business affairs, and although I didn't miss those challenges, Frank no longer had his consultant and confidante, but I never realized that loss to him. I saw my own life only.

"In retrospect, Frank put up with a lot from me, and so did the kids. I had limitations as a wife, and also as a mother, but I chose not to acknowledge them, so of course they became all the worse for being disavowed. It wasn't until I was a widow living alone that I began to perceive how difficult I must have been for others to put up with. Oh, yes," Sabrina acknowledged with tears forming, "I was more than a bit sanctimonious, so sure that I had all answers and the rest of the world needed to learn from me."

"How did you come to realize that, if indeed it is true, which I doubt?" the loyal Sally asked.

Thanking Sally for her support with a smile, Sabrina answered ruefully, "The hard way. By aggravating my husband until my marriage was beyond repair, and by alienating my children. Now, I don't know how to approach either Karenna or Paul to try to make amends. When I try to sort out just how it all happened, I get so confused that I can't even follow my own thoughts. However, the one thing I have learned is that I need to straighten out my own life before I start in on anyone else's again."

"That sounds like a good end goal," Sally conceded, "but in the meantime even adult children need their mother. It seems to me that none of you know how to communicate your needs to one another," Sally offered.

"So what do I do, call everyone into a family therapy session?" Sabrina challenged, stung by Sally's comment. "Maybe with a long distance phone call, since Karenna is in Texas and Paul in California." Sabrina's voice had become shrill.

Sally asked gently, "Is that what you did with them, turn defensive and cold when you didn't know what to do?"

Again, Sally's words stung. This time Sabrina reverted to methods that had always worked for her. "What do you mean, cold? I'm telling you what the situation is. I'm just being realistic. I'm *not* cold."

"Don't be angry, please," Sally reassured Sabrina. "All I'm doing is pointing out that all families have pretty poor records when it comes to positive communication. Believe me, I speak from experience, as you well know. You've heard me lament plenty about my family issues. A lot of misery goes uncorrected when it really could be made better. There are ways. But for now, let's just let it rest. Tell me, what do you have planned for Francisco when he comes?"

The break in dealing with the past provided the relief

Sabrina needed, and she was delighted to turn to a happy subject. Francisco had always worshipped her. He had never turned on her the way Frank and her children had. Maybe, she mused, that was because Francisco had never lived with her day in and day out, so he truly didn't know her the same way. Perhaps she and Francisco would become just as alienated if they did establish a long term relationship now. That gave her pause for thought before she answered Sally.

"We really don't have any plans yet," Sabrina admitted. I'm going to meet him at the airport, and we'll take it from there."

"Will you stay at the airport, or go into Cleveland, or come back to your house, or what? How long is he going to be here?"

"I really haven't thought that far ahead," Sabrina confessed. "I'll just see what happens. We have so much catching up to do. I know he'll be staying for a few days. I guess I better make reservations for him somewhere."

"Why don't you invite him to stay with you?" Sally was surprised at herself for suggesting this, since she still had doubts about the integrity of Francisco's intentions "Why should he stay somewhere else and have to commute back and forth when you have so much to talk about and not a lot of time?"

That thought startled Sabrina. What would the neighbors say? Was the house presentable? What if the kids found out? *Hell*, she thought quickly to herself, *who cares?* She started laughing, then explained the train of thought that had just barreled through her head.

"I like your conclusion," Sally affirmed. "Do what's best for you, not anyone else. Call me just before he comes in," Sally commanded. "You're going to need a little calming down." Sally truly hoped that Sabrina's heart would not be rent asunder again.

That night Sabrina again tried to call Paul and Karenna. She did not intend to tell them about the upcoming visit from a man they had never heard of, but she did want to hear her children's voices before her past came back to visit her. Or haunt her? Sabrina felt as terrified as he had even been in her life, but at both Paul's and Karenna's homes, she heard only their answering machines.

TEN

The following Tuesday morning, Sabrina awakened at five o'clock. Knowing she would never get back to sleep on this day, she puttered around the house, rearranging fresh cut flowers in the kitchen and straightening the tablecloth in the dining room as she pondered every possible outcome she could conjure into her imagination. Maybe Francisco would get sick and not come today, and she would have to go through this agony again. Maybe the plane would crash. Maybe he would find her heavier than he remembered and be disgusted. Her mind flew madly with possibilities until she finally forced herself to stop.

"Enough," she finally chided herself, "stop this nonsense. Take today one step at a time, and stop trying to anticipate every 'what if'."

Francisco was due to arrive on the 10:10 AM flight from Newark. Sabrina now had precisely two hours and forty-seven minutes before that moment, an event that was creating more butterflies in her stomach than even her wedding day had engendered.

She forced herself to finish her cup of tea, vacuumed the living room for the fourth time in two days, and finally decided that she could at last get dressed. The night before, after a dozen changes, she had ultimately chosen a chic navy pantsuit and plum colored V neck silk blouse that had amplifying folds to enhance the abundance of her bustline, which she noted had increased significantly since college days. The day before she had been to the salon for a touch up on her hair coloring, and she had managed to lose two pounds in the days since Francisco's call. *'Good'* was her conclusion, as she looked in the mirror one last time, then gathered her keys and started the car.

Traffic was light on I-480. Arriving at the airport in less than forty minutes, Sabrina immediately went to look at the incoming flight screen and gave a sigh of relief to see that the flight from Newark was expected on time. Taking a deep breath, she sat down and closed her eyes. Forty years. What would he look like? How would he react when he saw her? What would they do?

At 10:05 AM she got as close to his arrival gate as she could get. Finally, the flight was announced and Sabrina waited with bated breath as passengers began streaming up the walkway.

An elderly woman was brought up in a wheelchair, and a flight attendant accompanied a child until the party meeting the little girl was found. Then other passengers came, one by one being met by happy friends and family. Finally the crew came. Sabrina hastened forward to ask if anyone else were still on the plane.

"No, Ma'am. We're the last off the flight. You might check with the desk to see if your party got diverted for some reason."

With a leaden heart, Sabrina returned to the airline's information desk to ask what might have happened. "Excuse me. I was expecting someone on the flight arriving from Newark. His name is …"

"Francisco del Oro" she heard behind her.

She spun around, and there he was. Her Francisco, slender and elegant and so very, very handsome. Automatically, she put out her arms, and suddenly they were together as one, just as it should always have been.

"Cara Mia. I booked an earlier flight because I simply could not wait to start on my way to see you. Of course, that flight ended up being delayed and I just arrived at a different runway."

Sabrina could not say anything. She closed her eyes, then opened them again. He was still there, smiling the smile that only he had, and he was dabbing at her face with a fine silk handkerchief.

"Come on, Darling. Let's go get some breakfast. I couldn't eat before I came because I was too nervous." He laughed that Francisco laugh, and Sabrina was transported back to her college days again.

Hand in hand, they walked out of the airport toward her car as Sabrina began to pull herself back together. "Francisco, I have so much to explain. Please be patient with me."

He pulled her to himself again. "Beloved, we will take all the time in the world. There is no more hurry for anything, ever again. We will gradually grow together just as we once were, and nothing will ever separate us, I swear to you."

Over breakfast, they brought each other superficially up to date on their respective families. Sabrina again expressed her condolences on Francisco's recent loss of his wife. She could tell by the way he spoke that theirs had been a strong and deep bond, but Sabrina felt it was based on friendship and mutual respect far more than on fiery love. In turn, Sabrina briefly told of Frank's death, and her return to Ohio. She barely talked about her three children, while Francisco talked enthusiastically about his two daughters and four sons.

Returning to her house, Sabrina fixed coffee with lots of sugar, remembering how he liked it. They went to sit in the sun room at the back of the house and gradually Sabrina began to expand on what she had revealed to Francisco, starting with the early days of her marriage. Francisco listened attentively, never interrupting her.

"Frank and I remained in Chicago for several years," Sabrina began. "However, as his business grew, so did his reputation. He was encouraged to run for political office, but he always turned down the offers. He hated political life, and he knew I felt the same. Then he started receiving offers to head national associations. Eventually he accepted a position based in Washington, D.C. Our son Paul objected vehemently, but both the girls were excited. We moved to the Virginia suburbs, just outside of Washington, in the mid seventies. Shortly after we arrived, there was the hostage crisis in Iran, and the mood of the country became more conservative. That suited Frank just fine, since his politics had always been pretty cautious anyway. His office was in the District, in a swanky building with lots of high billing attorneys, powerful associations, that kind of tenant. He loved lobbying on the Hill, at which he became very proficient. The power he developed in Washington intoxicated him, and he was very happy."

"The girls adapted quickly to their new environment, and eventually Paul stopped grousing about the friends he had been force to leave behind in Chicago. However, Paul had conflicts with his teachers, so Frank decided to enroll him in a nearby boarding school. It seemed a good decision at the time, but now I wonder. I think Paul felt abandoned, even though we lived close enough that he could come home on weekends. I made sure that I was at his school a lot. In fact, I was there so frequently that I became like a second mother to a lot of the boys who didn't have family nearby. It was funny, the other kids seemed to like me a lot better than my own son did, which was the same thing that had happened between my mother and me."

Here Sabrina paused for a moment, realizing what she had just said. Francisco just squeezed her hand and after a moment, she resumed her story.

"We lived in Virginia for the next twenty years. While the children were at home, we always decorated the house lavishly at Christmas and everyone would have friends over. The same thing happened for birthday parties, Russian holidays, you name it, any excuse would do to have a celebration. The Olensky household came to be known as the social center for all the teenagers in the neighborhood. If a child did not get home in time for dinner, the parents knew to call our house first." Sabrina chuckled at the memory of one parent calling her to complain vehemently about how her children preferred to be over at Sabrina's house rather than at their own home. If the tone of voice Sabrina heard was typical of how that woman treated her kids, it was no wonder, she thought.

"Paul did not participate in the socializing so much, since he was away at school, but Karenna and Sarah each had their own set of friends. Of course, there was squabbling when they both wanted a sleepover the same weekend or something like that. Karenna usually won. Not only was she a few years older, which she thought gave her special privileges, but she was also a lot more aggressive. Little Sarah was quiet, and her friends were vastly different from Karenna's."

"There were some incidents with Karenna's friends that we should have paid more attention to. Sometimes valuable things would go missing from our house. I remember once when the police found a silver picture frame that had encased a picture of Frank's grandfather in a pawn shop. The police said that it had been part of a bunch of loot pawned by Karenna's best friend, who was later sent to a drug rehab center. Karenna herself went to juvenile court more than once for possessing marijuana, but Frank's influence always managed to get her sentence reduced to probation. At one point, I insisted that Frank and I attend a family therapy group called Tough Love to learn how to deal with her, but Frank stopped after a couple of sessions."

This time Francisco did break in. "Sabrina, my beloved Sabrina, you are such a good woman. How did these things happen?" he asked. Francisco was incredulous that someone like his beloved Sabrina could have a drug addict for a daughter.

"They do. We always sprang to her defense, never let her be accountable for her behavior. There would always be an excuse for what happened, and frequently either Frank and sometimes even I would be the originator of the excuse. She never had to learn that behaviors have consequences, and that people have to be responsible for themselves. It was largely our fault, because we never wanted her to suffer. There was also the issue that if Karenna went to a juvenile facility, that would have been a disgrace to Frank," Sabrina added, a touch of anger in her voice.

"Finally, Karenna graduated from high school, and was accepted at Wellesley. One thing Frank always insisted on was excellent academic performance, and indeed, he got it from all three of his kids. He managed to keep Karenna's drug record quiet, and Wellesley thought they were getting someone spectacular because she was nearly a straight A student in tough subjects as well as a leader in debate club, an actress in school plays, and a statewide recognized athlete."

"What about Sarah? Was she the same kind of student?" Francisco inquired.

"Sarah was an enigma. She loved playing the violin in the high school orchestra, singing a capella with the city choral group and painting landscapes. On the other hand, her favorite subjects in high school were advanced math and chemistry, which I never thought matched up with artistic things, but now psychologists say that music and math and science all draw on the same parts of the brain. On weekends she would love to go hiking in the Shenandoahs. She begged Frank for more than two years to be allowed to take scuba diving lessons, until he finally relented and bought Sarah her own gear. She was never interested in skiing or tennis or horseback riding, which most other children coveted. She always found her own projects to follow."

Suddenly, Sabrina stopped talking. She glanced over at Francisco and apologized in what sounded to Francisco as an unapologetic manner.

"I'm so sorry, Francisco," she said in an almost stony voice. "I've been chattering on and on and not letting you talk. Please tell me more about your family."

Realizing that Sabrina had come to some sort of serious break in her thoughts, Francisco began to talk of when he finally decided to make his life back home in Peru. He had allowed his parents to select a wife for him, since he no longer cared about having a love match. Fortunately, his parents had chosen well.

"Angelica was a college graduate who was well versed in history and sociology. She loved to participate in high level social functions. She was warm and personable, and utterly compassionate. Over the years, we had six children, four of whom graduated from college. The oldest daughter married right out of high school and she now has three kids of her own. Her husband makes a good living for the family and she seems perfectly content. My second daughter went to art school, although I did not approve at the time. As it turned out, she is extremely talented, and now has her own studio. She earns more money than any of my boys," he added with a chuckle.

"We want what is best for our children," Sabrina observed, "even though we don't know what that is any better than they do. Why doesn't that ever stop us from trying to direct their lives?"

"Well, sometimes parents do know best," Francisco responded heatedly. "My oldest son wanted to run off with a dancer when he was twenty, and I threatened him with disinheritance. He straightened out, finished college, and is now well employed, although he still does foolish things that I have to bail him out of once in a while. Maybe, from what you have said, though, I ought to let him find his own way out of trouble."

After a moment's pause, Francisco continued. "Anyway, from four college graduates, one artist and one happy housewife, I have nine grandchildren, and my first great grandchild expected in a few weeks. What more can a man want?" Looking at Sabrina, Francisco answered himself. *I want you, my beloved Sabrina.*

ELEVEN

Francisco insisted that Sabrina not cook for him, so at dinner in an out of the way restaurant where Sabrina was sure no one would interrupt their precious moments together, Sabrina and Francisco agreed to tell each other stories about some of the most memorable occurrences that had happened to each of them since they had last seen one another. Francisco insisted that Sabrina go first. She reflected for a moment, then a smile began to dance across her face.

"This will be a long story," she warned, "because there is a lot leading up to it. It is a story about Paul, and this particular incident brought me more joy than just about anything else in my relationship with my son. I was so proud of him then, so hopeful that he had turned an important corner and become someone with confidence and surety about himself." Sabrina paused for a moment. "How I wish that feeling of confidence could be rekindled. I guess there are so many 'if only's' in our lives. In this case, if only the story could have continued on the same course it all seemed to be heading for a short while."

Francisco settled himself comfortably into his chair, put his chin in his hands and prepared to listen. Being in the presence of Sabrina was still beyond his comprehension, and he expected to wake up at any moment back in his office in Lima, finalizing deals with government officials. Gradually, her voice lulled him, as she began her account of the milestone with Paul.

As she had warned, the telling did take a long time, but it told him volumes about who she had become. It also frightened him a bit, as he began to realize that the woman sitting across from him was no longer quite the same Sabrina he had loved so blindly in college. She had evolved, changed, become different. Not worse, not better, just different.

As he listened, he wondered if their lives had taken them in such different directions that it would be impossible to return to what they had known long ago. Suddenly he realized that he too had changed, in his ideas, his feelings, his strongly held beliefs. This was a contingency he had never considered before. For the past forty years he had unshakably believed that Sabrina would always be the core of his life, and that someday they would be reunited. But as she told her story, he began to understand that she had experienced forty years of living outside his world, as, of course, he had likewise lived outside hers. Would it be possible to re-establish where they had once been? He was momentarily stunned by his doubts.

"Paul was about seventeen," Sabrina began, "in his junior year at the academy in Fairfax. He was on the swim team, but only as a fill-in if the varsity man could not compete that day. That irked him something awful, and he was always complaining when he came home on weekends. At school, though, he would put on a bright face and pretend to be perfectly content to be a substitute swimmer helping his school team when needed. As his mother, however, I saw both demeanors.

"Paul didn't have a lot of friends to hang around with, even though he tried hard to fit in. In contrast to Frank's magnetic personality, Paul just couldn't intermingle productively. I always wondered if he felt there was no way he could compete with his father, so he deliberately didn't try. He would join sports teams, but never do quite well enough. He would inevitably find something to pick a fight about whenever someone really tried to befriend him. I think he was very, very lonely.

"There was one boy, though. His name was Emanuel. This kid followed Paul around like a puppy dog, never being put off by Paul's roughness. Emanuel was a scholarship student from somewhere out in the southwest. I think it was

Arizona, maybe. Because Emanuel's parents didn't have a lot of money, over single week vacations Emanuel usually had to stay in Virginia. Once in a while, Paul would invite him to our house.

"Emanuel was a tall, gangly teenager, with a pimply face and a bit of a nasal voice. The wealthy boys made fun of him because he couldn't participate in a lot of the socializing that went on. They also rejected him because he always got the best grades. Paul remained neutral, not making fun of him but also never defending him. Somehow Paul thought that was being fair, no matter how many times I tried to explain that it was really being cruel. He just would not listen. In truth, Emanuel was the center of much of Paul's unbounded complaining. Paul would fuss endlessly that 'Pimple Face' would never leave him alone, but as his mother, I understood that he was actually grateful for the adoration.

"Seeing how isolated Paul was, I tried to do what I could to make him more socially acceptable with the groups of kids he wanted to be a part of. I would invite some of the boys for a Saturday afternoon of horseback riding at the local stable, or drive them to a Redskins game on a Sunday afternoon. Frequently I would just happen to show up at school when I knew that someone Paul wanted to be on good terms with had a special need. That wasn't hard to find out because I had an 'in' with the front office people and heard a lot of the gossip.

"Then one day it struck me that I had turned into my mother, always trying to shape the landscape for my child's benefit, and not allowing him to learn on his own behalf. When I recognized what I was doing, I decided to stop being such an eternal presence at the school. The headmaster, of course, had no idea what was going on, and he kept pestering me to organize the Christmas ball, as I had for the previous two holiday seasons. When I told him that I wouldn't be able to this year, he bribed me. He told me that if I would organize the ball, he would see to it that Paul would get special dispensation to go on a trip he wanted, even though he had not qualified academically.

"At first, I was shocked. However, I had been listening to Paul talk about how important this trip was to him for weeks. Certain members of the junior class were being selected, based on academic performance, to fly to London over spring break. For some reason, one of the few subjects Paul had really showed an interest in was English history, and he really wanted to go.

"Meanwhile, several things were going on at home, both with Frank and with each child individually. Frank had unexpectedly been invited to head an economic delegation to the Soviet Union for the purpose of developing better trade ties. As leader of one of the more formidable trade organizations in Washington, he had been instrumental in lobbying for some very important national legislation that encouraged international economic dealings. The President of the United States had personally asked Frank to return to his homeland as an example of the power of capitalism. Frank was very proud of this honor, and of course, wanted his wife to go along to see him in all his glory. He insisted that, for once, I forego involvement with school stuff and go with him.

"However, at the same time, a lot of things were happening. My mother was pressuring both Frank and me to buy Paul a computer, which she was sure would boost his academic performance. Her argument was that Frank had insisted on Paul's taking difficult courses, and therefore Frank had an obligation to provide his son with all the tools necessary to ensure his success. Frank refused to go along with his mother-in-law's demand. That was back in the early eighties when computers were still a relatively new phenomenon and their value seemed questionable. Mom, in her inimitable style, went behind our backs and bought Paul a computer, and Frank was furious.

"To add to the strain, Karenna came down with mononucleosis, which meant she was home from school for weeks and barely had enough energy to sit up in bed to study an hour a day. Meanwhile, Sarah had developed a mad crush on her sixth grade geography teacher. With all of this going on, I decided that I could not fly off to the other side of the world. Frank did not take it very well at all when I told him I wouldn't go, and when he left, he told me I better have things straightened out by the time he got home.

"If I had been anywhere near smart, I would have told the headmaster to find someone else to be that year's organizer, but I didn't. Frank had gone off overseas in high dudgeon and there I was, left on my own for ten days with one physically sick child, another love sick child and a third furious child. I tried to appease the furious child by agreeing to the headmaster's coercion.

"Paul, of course, did not know about the deal I had made with the headmaster, and he was still fretting and grumbling about how he had barely missed the GPA he needed, how it was the teacher's fault because there was a trick question on the exam that no one should have been expected to know, how he had a really bad stomachache that day, and on and on."

Francisco broke in. "Is Paul still such a complainer?" he asked, almost in anger.

Sabrina laughed bitterly. "Not to me. Today he barely even speaks to me. I'll get a card on most of my birthdays, maybe a two minute phone call on Mother's Day, and an expensive but utterly irrelevant gift at Christmas. When I call him at work, his secretary rarely puts me through, and he always has his answering machine on at home to screen unwanted calls. I keep hoping that things will change, but now I know how my mother felt when I cut her out of my life."

Francisco was amazed that his Sabrina, and indeed, the boy's father Frank, had allowed this type of behavior to continue. If he had been Paul's father, it would have been different, he knew. He could see that his once joyful Sabrina had become embittered, although she tried hard to disguise it. She was no longer the carefree lover of life he had known in college, but had instead become a somewhat cynical woman who had lost her *joie d'vivre*. His heart wheezed in sympathy, and in sadness. Life could take so many cruel turns.

"I'm sorry, I interrupted your story," he apologized. "Please go on. But I haven't heard anything joyous yet."

"Well, I'm getting to that part. Believe me, this story definitely marks one of the highlights of my experiences with Paul."

Francisco looked at Sabrina a little quizzically, since it certainly did not appear to be anything like a highlight, but he decided to be patient and see how the story turned out.

Sabrina smiled at him affectionately and resumed. "I arranged for some spectacular entertainment at the Christmas Ball, which of course was known as the Winter Dance to take account of everyone's religious preferences. Being a highly respected non-sectarian school, there were enrollees from many faiths, so the word Christmas could not be used.

"I managed to talk the U.S. Secretary of the Treasury, who had graduated from the Academy umpteen years before, into being our guest speaker. Several other renowned alumni returned for the dance, and donations skyrocketed, which had been the headmaster's intention, of course. He was delighted, and Paul's name got on the approved list for the spring break trip to England.

"Three months later, about ten days prior to departure, Paul was informed, and he was ecstatic. Meanwhile, I was feeling like a prostitute who had sold her talents to buy something Paul really did not deserve. Then one day he came home and wanted to talk to me privately. It had been years since he had made that kind of request, and I had no idea what was coming.

"'Mom,' he said, after closing the door to the library, 'I learned yesterday that you had arranged the Christmas thing as a deal with Dr. Berger so that I could go to London.' He paused when I opened my mouth to say something. 'No, don't deny it. I know it's true. What I wanted to tell you is -- well, thanks. I really appreciate your trying to do something like that for me.'

"Again I tried to say something, but he just plowed right on. 'I also know how much trouble you got into with Dad when he wanted you to go to the Soviet Union with him, but instead you stayed here to take care of me and the girls. I started thinking about how many times you had done stuff like that, and how rarely I notice it. I just wanted you to know that this time I did see it.'

"Well, I was flabbergasted, and then Paul came out with something that absolutely floored me. 'You did something really selfless, and that challenged me. I thought about it a lot and decided that I, too, can think of other people, not just myself all the time. I wanted everyone to know that I am your son and how proud I am of that.'

"By then, you could have swept me up with a feather duster. I was so dumfounded that I couldn't speak, so I just continued to listen, probably with my mouth hanging wide open.

"'Mom,' he said, 'you know that Emanuel had good grades, but couldn't come up with the money to afford this trip. I went to Dr. Berger and asked him to give my ticket and hotel reservations to Emanuel. I'm going to give him the Christmas checks Gramma and Gramps sent me so he will have some decent spending money. Don't try to talk me out of it. It's already done.'

"Then he got up and walked out of the room. I guess he didn't want to argue with me, because he thought I would tell him to go to London anyway, and I would pay for Emanuel, which is probably exactly what I would have done at that instant. So I sat there for several minutes, digesting what my son had resolved to do, then I broke down crying. Later that night when I had composed myself, I went to his room and told him how very, very proud I was of him."

"If he behaved so admirably then, why doesn't he still?" Francisco asked, puzzlement furrowing his brow.

"Well, if that had been the end of the story, perhaps Paul would have maintained his changed behavior. But for some reason, happy endings seem to elude him." Sabrina bent her head in sorrow and said nothing for several minutes. Eventually, she went on, now speaking in a monotone.

"The group left for England, about twenty of them all together. They had a marvelous time visiting the important sights -- Westminster Abbey, Big Ben, the Tower of London, Downing Street, all those places - and they went shopping at Harrods and places on Fleet Street. On the next to last day of the trip, some of the students took a side trip to Stonehenge.

"Emanuel was among the group that went to Stonehenge. Exactly what happened that day has never been clear, even though Scotland Yard investigated it very thoroughly. The story that came back to the United States was that a psycho claiming a grudge against space aliens entering our world through a portal in Stonehenge suddenly opened fire with a machine gun, and several tourists were shot. Emanuel was among those hit. His classmates were really spooked, since Emanuel was the only student injured, although they had all been standing together.

"At first it didn't seem too bad. They got him to a hospital where he immediately underwent surgery. Then during the operation, his heart just stopped beating. The doctors worked hard to resuscitate him, but he never regained consciousness. He died on the operating table.

"His body was flown back to Virginia, then on to Arizona where his parents held a private funeral. Paul went to the service in Arizona and talked to Emanuel's parents. They said it was just one of those things that happen in life, but Paul could never accept that. To this day, Paul carries Emanuel's death in his heart, and, unfortunately, in his mind. He has twisted the truth all around so that now he has convinced himself that his attempt to show goodness was not acceptable to whatever higher power there is, that Emanuel's death occurred because he, Paul, was not worthy to be gracious to someone else. He believes that he is such a valueless person because of his years of self centeredness that nothing he does now can ever offset his depravity."

"But that doesn't make sense," Francisco exclaimed.

"Of course it doesn't, not to anyone but Paul. We sent him to a psychiatrist who did nothing but give him medication, and then to a psychologist who told him that he needed to grow up and stop making himself the center of the world. She told him that he really wasn't so important that a spiritual being would punish him in this way. After that, he refused any more mental health treatment.

""He got himself into a profession where he works with numbers and data, not people, so that his unfitness does not totally incapacitate him. To this day, he remains a horridly miserable human being. He has been through two marriages, and once was taken to court for beating someone up after a minor car accident. I have tried, I can't tell you how many times, to steer him back into therapy, but he simply won't go."

How do we guide our children on the right path, Francisco wondered. *How do we help them when they fall so deep into a well of misery that they cannot see any way out?* He reached over and pulled Sabrina into himself, holding her sobbing body and whispering nonsense words into her hair as she cried until he thought it would never end. Others in the restaurant pretended not to notice.

TWELVE

"Beloved," he said softly, when the whimpering finally subsided, "you said that this was such a joyous story for you. The joy was so short lived. Is that how your life has been, just occasional glimpses of happiness, followed by such melancholy?"

Sabrina straightened herself and told Francisco that it was now his turn to tell a story of a memorable event from his life. But first she answered his question, which chafed her because she felt that he had misread her entirely.

"Dearest Francisco," she assured him. "My life has been filled with beauty and joy, just not all the time. No one's is. The reason I hold the memory of that time so dear is because I saw, however briefly, what I always knew about my son, that a part of him is good, self sacrificing and solicitous. He is a wonderful person, and his reality is far different from the annoying, sometimes menacing persona he shows to the public. His first wife Patricia saw that, but his anger eventually overcame even her ability to bring out the goodness. I truly do believe that some day he will allow himself to acknowledge his decency again. I pray that it will be during my lifetime."

Francisco digested that for a moment, and felt his love for Sabrina flow into the heavens. Again he realized that this was a woman with a remarkable ability to see good in people even when others couldn't. After a moment, he began his own first memorable story, telling her of a conference he had attended with the Presidents and Economic Ministers from several Latin American countries. At this conference he had been invited to present a theory he had developed whose implementation eventually led to a breakthrough in regional economics.

"I really made an impact on the thinking of some very hard-headed economists who were sure that the long standing policies of their own countries were the only way to do business. At this gathering, I was able to persuade people to look beyond their own borders and instead see how regional cooperation could enhance not only their own productivity, but that of their neighbors as well."

Francisco went on to explain how his presentation had not been well received, which was no surprise to him. However, through later meetings with the individual policy makers of each country represented at the conference, Francisco explained and re-explained how co-operation could positively impact each country's trade. In the one-on-one sessions, he made more headway, and even though his initiatives were not overtly accepted at that convention, over the next few years, many of his concepts began to show up in various negotiations.

"So your contribution had an eventual impact on millions of people," Sabrina observed proudly. "Indeed, thanks to you, Francisco, it seems that throughout Central and South America, there is now a more efficient method of food distribution and better concepts of transportation. You made a tremendous difference, not only for your own country but for your continent. I'm so proud of you," she said as she smiled at him with great affection. Briefly she wondered why she had never heard Francisco's name on national news broadcasts, before remembering how provincial American news coverage was, even now at the turn into the twenty-first century.

Francisco laughed deprecatingly. "Don't make me out to be the benefactor of the southern hemisphere," he pled. "Mankind has to advance all the time, and all I did was produce an idea that others eventually decided might work."

They arrived back at Sabrina's house just as a thunderstorm began battering the windows and lightning lit up the sky. As well as catching up on the past, Sabrina and Francisco also had a desperate need to explore the here and now. Without verbal communication, they had earlier implicitly understood that Francisco would stay at Sabrina's house, and they now walked back to her bedroom, pausing for deep kisses along the way. Although nervous at first, they quickly fell back into the gentle and sweet lovemaking of their youth, massaging each others' bodies and remembering where and how each especially liked to be touched. They listened to the rain pounding the roof, and they both felt totally safe. They made love an exhausting three times, delighted with their stamina despite their age.

"We can't do this every night," Francisco joyfully complained. "I'll never live to see another birthday."

"Wanna bet?" Sabrina asked, snuggling down into Francisco's shoulder and sighing blissfully.

The next morning, thunderous rumbling portended a full day of heavy rain, so that day they did not bother to go out. Just before noon, the electricity went off and they lit a fire. Sabrina straightened out two wire hangers and they toasted marshmallows, with Sabrina teaching Francisco the delight of indulging in s'mores. "Graham crackers, two squares of Hershey chocolate, and two melted marshmallows,' she instructed. "You have to melt the marshmallows slowly, not burn them," she admonished as Francisco's caught on fire. "Slow and easy, kinda like us," she teased.

"Licking his fingers noisily, Francisco stated pompously,

"The next time I have a high level meeting with ambassadors, I shall insist on these for dessert, clothes hangers and all."

Sabrina giggled. "You don't have high level meetings with ambassadors anymore, remember? You're retired."

"Oh." Francisco almost sounded as if this had been a revelation to him. "Then that means all the more for me," he pronounced, putting two more marshmallows on his hanger and sticking it back into the blaze.

"Tell me your second story," Francisco prompted.

Sabrina thought for a moment, nodded to herself that she could finally share this one, and began slowly. "The second memorable event of my life probably started with a scene something like where we are right now," Sabrina said, sadness tingeing her voice. "People were sitting around a campfire, telling stories and probably enjoying s'mores. Except that time it was Sarah and a group of her friends when she was twenty-one years old. She had been invited to participate in a two week hiking trip through the Rockies. Sarah had been hiking for years, ever since she earned a badge as a Girl Scout. The organizers were renowned hikers, so we encouraged her to accept the invitation. Besides, she was twenty-one years old and certainly did not need her parents' permission.

"She promised to call us every other night to tell us where she was and what the weather was like. The first few calls were normal, with Sarah sounding very excited and happy about the boundless beauty of the rugged Western mountains. Most of her hiking before that had been in the Shenandoahs and Appalachians, so this was definitely a new experience for her. She just couldn't get over how clear the skies were at night, and she assured us that she and her friends were having a 'splendiferous time'." Sabrina paused. "She loved that word, splendiferous, and whenever she used it, we knew that she was describing something that was totally new to her experience of life.

"Then one night, Frank and I had just come back from a Picasso exhibition at the Smithsonian when we heard the phone ringing. We almost ignored it, since we were trying to carry some packages in with us. But by intuition, perhaps, I grabbed the phone in the basement and juggled the packages into my other arm. Sarah's best friend Debbie was sobbing at the other end of the line.

"Mrs. Olensky," she said, "I'm sorry. I have to tell you something."

"At that instant, I felt a chill come over me that has never completely thawed," Sabrina whispered. Gathering back her strength, she went on. "Debbie explained that there had been a bear attack at their camp two hours before, and that Sarah and one other girl had been badly mauled. Both young women had been rushed to the nearest hospital by ambulance.

"A few minutes later a park ranger called us to tell us the same thing. He was concerned that someone else had called us first, since he felt that it was his duty to notify family members in this kind of situation. Sometimes, he said, civilians were too upset to explain things properly. He kept us on the line for quite a while to be sure we were not hysterical, and I will always remember his kindness and concern. He offered to make flight arrangements for us, but we already had. The ranger met us at the airport and stayed with us the whole time we were out there in Colorado.

"He took us to the hospital, and I was shocked when I saw my child. Her face was unrecognizable. The attending physician told us that the bear had first swiped her left cheek, then continued to maul her so that they had to give her multiple transfusions to restore her blood volume. How she was still alive when we got there is beyond my comprehension, other than her own determination to say goodbye to her parents. Our beautiful Sarah died a few hours after we arrived at the hospital."

Sabrina stopped talking and almost stopped breathing as she relived this agony for the millionth time. Finally, she went on. "One of her friends had been badly injured, but eventually recovered. The parents of that girl told us that their daughter must have been a better person than Sarah."

"Oh, my God," Francisco moaned in sympathy. "How

could they?"

"Their own pain, I guess. I don't know. At the memorial service we held for Sarah, teachers and friends and people we didn't even know spoke about Sarah's spirit and how she had inspired them. Everyone wanted us to know that her presence here on earth had had a profound impact on their lives, and that they were grateful we had raised such a child. The conflict of feelings between great pride and incomprehensible sorrow was overwhelming. I was numb. Without Frank and the children, I would have stopped living right then and there, I know. I considered suicide several times in the weeks after that, but I was always too afraid to try."

Neither Francisco nor Sabrina spoke for a while. Finally Sabrina mumbled, "So that is my second memorable incident," Now what about yours?" Somehow she had to turn away from those devastating memories, for which her two remaining children continued to blame her. Somehow, she felt, Paul and Karenna forgot they had all been brought up to embrace life fully. Camping had been part of Sarah's life for years, and Sabrina was sure that there was nothing unreasonable about supporting Sarah's choice to enjoy an activity she loved. Sarah's sister and brother, however, argued vehemently that their mother should have been more protective, that she should have known there were dangers, and that she should have prevented this accident which took their baby sister away from them.

Francisco murmured softly. "I have nothing to say right now. Let's go sit on the porch and watch the storm."

They sat there on the back porch, where Sabrina and her parents had perched themselves many times, where she had quivered the night she was raped, where so much of her life had passed. They looked out over the lake and watched the lightning dance shadows across the small waves. When it became too cool, Francisco went back inside and brought out a comforter to put around Sabrina, and they sat together in silence until darkness arrived.

"Let's eat, Beloved."

Sabrina shook her head. "Not quite yet. I'm still remembering."

Some time later, maybe five minutes, or maybe a couple of hours, she wasn't sure, she said, "I will tell you the third miracle of my life. The first two stories are miracles, they truly are. Perhaps they are what led me to the third miracle." And she began the story of her soul's quest for an understanding of what had become of her life.

"I was brought up an Episcopalian, as you well remember. You and I used to have expansive discussions about the differences between your Catholicism, about which you seemed to have a great understanding, and my Episcopalianism, about which I knew very little other than the Sunday rituals. I really did not understand much at all about Christianity, other than that I called myself a Christian because that was what I was called by my family and people around me.

"It always annoyed me when one branch of Christianity would hold itself to be better or wiser or more holy than another, or when a Christian would put down a Hindu or a Muslim just because the had been brought up in a different culture. My freshman year, you probably remember that I took that comparative religion course and wrote my term paper on Islam, which I was amazed to find had beliefs and traditions that were just as powerful as the ones I had been brought up with.

"Well, I stopped attending the Episcopal church. Indeed, for a long time I stopped believing in God at all, because He had allowed such a terrible thing as rape to happen to me. I held Him directly responsible for human behavior.

"Then one day when I was living in Vincennes, I was eating lunch in a park. It was springtime and I enjoyed sitting outside to eat and read a magazine during my lunch hour. My workmates understood that I sometimes wanted to be alone, and they would not bother me unless I specifically asked someone to join me.

"One day I was sitting there, and I guess I was staring off into space. Nearby was a teenager who had also been reading, but at the moment she was sitting with her eyes closed. She opened them just as I glanced over at her, and she smiled a smile that was so genuine and untroubled that I asked her to please come join me. We got to talking, and I was astonished at the insight she demonstrated about so many things. Her wisdom was truly far beyond her apparent years. Amazingly, her thinking was unsullied by anger or prejudice or self pity, which is unusual for anyone, let alone a teenager.

"I don't know how, but as we talked, the topic of religion came up. I expressed my dissatisfaction with the misery I saw all around me, and she reminded me that God gave us the rules to live by, along with the free will to comply with or reject those rules. She reminded me that we humans have the capacity to understand what is right and wrong. If we harm others, that is our own responsibility, not God's.

"I guess that really took me by surprise. I had never looked at it that way before. Yes, I knew we had the Ten Commandments and all that, but I had never put it together with personal responsibility before. Somehow that link had just never clicked in my mind. I thought that people who lived by the Bible did so because God chose certain chosen individuals to be like that. It was the first time that I had really considered that we all have the same teachings to start with, and it is how we individually apply them that makes a difference.

"Well, that got me going, big time. I went to the library and started reading about religions in general, and was surprised to find that the theological teachings of Judaism and Christianity and Islam were pretty much the same. You know -- acknowledge that there is only one God, love that one God so that your heart will be open to accept His love for you, strive toward personal excellence in order to better understand what God expects of humanity, do right by your neighbor, that kind of stuff. I learned that it was social teachings that differed from one religion to another, such as laws about divorce, forbidden foods, use of alcohol, etc. However, the basic theological teachings were unchanged from one faith to another, and I began to wonder what that meant.

"Gradually, I came back to having a slightly more comfortable existence with God, and my quest for understanding went on. I visited several different churches, becoming what I guess is known as a shopper. Interestingly, one Sunday morning a minister gave his sermon on people who went from church to church looking for what they considered the 'best deal'. He made it quite clear that he did not want such personages in his congregation. His attitude was clearly that if someone did not accept his version of the truth, then they could go away and not bother to come back. I ran into that attitude quite a bit, actually, in several churches I visited around town. Most denominations did not seem to welcome questions.

"I was becoming discouraged again. I felt that there had to be some faith out there that would allow people to ask questions until they felt they had the answers they needed. Then one day I saw this young girl in the park again, and I asked her what her religious background was. At first, she was a bit reluctant to talk with me, not because she did not want to share her faith, but because her faith discouraged proselytization. After I asked for some specifics, however, she invited me to a meeting that Friday night. She said she would be happy to come by to pick me up, and I gave her my work address.

"That evening, I was introduced to a faith that encouraged people to see common threads among all religions, to include everyone in their lives, not just people who had the same skin color or economic background. I told Samantha, that was her name, that I wanted to learn more. She promised to bring me some books the following week, and she did. Whatever she said she would do, she always did, and so did others from the group she was with. There was no show, no pretense. They just believed in fulfilling obligations, doing what was right, living honorably. Before that, I had encountered plenty of 'religious' people who talked the talk, but didn't very often walk the walk. These people were different.

"I met her parents and one of her sisters at subsequent meetings. She told me that another sister did not accept the faith, but there was no attitude of condemnation. She explained that each person has to come to an understanding and acceptance on their own. Husbands could not force wives to believe a certain way, parents could not force children, ministers could not force congregations. By example and by teaching, people of this faith demonstrated their beliefs. Those who chose to accept were welcomed; those who did not were likewise welcome to continue asking questions."

In the background, thunder reverberated and lightning bared the far reaches of the sky. Sabrina and Francisco sat there, in a moment of honesty and inner serenity that absorbed the fury of nature and fortified their togetherness. Francisco, too, had heard of such a faith, but had not followed through to learn more about it. Was God speaking to them tonight? Did God actually do such things for individuals? Were the spirits of certain individuals drawn to a quest for God? Why wasn't everyone's? These thoughts racked his mind as he held his beloved Sabrina tightly against him, protecting her from the wrath of the storm as well as the passion of her own emotions.

"Did you become a member of that church?" he eventually asked.

"It wasn't a church, the way we think of organized churches. There was no clergy, no hierarchy. Individuals were responsible to investigate the truth of the teachings they heard. No one was considered an 'expert', ordained to pass on the religion to someone else. This concept really appealed to me because it was so different. I had begun to believe in personal responsibility, and I felt that it was important to have that same responsibility for my spiritual life as well as my material life.

Soon thereafter, however, I married and moved to Chicago, so I lost contact with those folks, but I always felt that their message had meaning for me that I have yet to fathom." Suddenly, she felt exhausted. "I'm too tired right now to complete this story," she said. "I definitely want to finish it, but could we do so later? Right now, I'm famished. There's a special restaurant I want to take you to."

The rain had let up, and they drove to a fancy restaurant in Cleveland where Sabrina was again sure she would not encounter any acquaintances. They shared a lovely, peaceful dinner with no interruptions, other than an overly solicitous waiter.

When they returned home, they headed directly to the bedroom and joyfully picked up where they had left off the night before, this time a little more slowly but just as passionately. Sabrina fell asleep on Francisco's shoulder, wondering dreamily if this was how life was now going to proceed for her.

THIRTEEN

Francisco planned to stay with Sabrina for eight days, following which he was expected to return to Peru for his first great grandchild's christening. Thus far, he and Sabrina had spent most of their time alone, with the exception of Thursday evening at the Spanish dance performance with Sally. To Sabrina's relief, Sally had quickly succumbed to Francisco's charms. By the end of the evening, Sally leaned over and whispered into Sabrina's ear, "All objections are withdrawn. This is a wonderful man for you. Hold on to him."

Now, on day six, the two of them had gone to visit Anna. To Sabrina's consternation, however, Anna was definitely not happy to meet this 'Cisco guy'. Even though Anna and Sabrina had talked on the phone before the meeting, with Sabrina assuring her sister that Francisco was a very nice man, somewhere inside herself, Anna remembered when Mommy and Daddy had talked about someone by that name. In her internal storage of feelings, Anna recalled that those discussions had created a lot of tension in her home, so when Sabrina introduced them, Anna did not meet Francisco's eyes. Instead, she muttered a very fast 'hi', then turned her back on Francisco and launched into telling Sabrina about a planned trip to Disney World for all eight of the group home residents.

"The county's gonna pay for half of the trip, and we gotta come up with money for the other half," Anna informed Sabrina. "Billy's mom gave some, and I think someone else's brother did, too. But you have to help," Anna insisted. "I been here the longest, so my family has to contribute most."

Sabrina recalled that four years before, a similar trip had been planned, with no county funding. On that occasion, Sabrina had been asked not only for a donation, but also to go along with the group home residents as a chaperone. That experience had convinced Sabrina that she would never to do something like that again. Dealing with Anna individually was no problem for Sabrina because they were sisters, but being one of only a couple of chaperones trying to watch over several impaired adults who were not willing to follow instructions from a virtual stranger was more than Sabrina was willing to undertake again. Recalling how difficult it had been, Sabrina momentarily wondered why this kind of trip was ever planned at all. As she thought more about it, however, Sabrina considered that she and her family had taken yearly vacations, and why shouldn't these residents have similar options. *Ah, we so called normal people forget how fortunate we are*, she thought to herself in a moment of humility. Although she knew that she herself would not chaperone again, she realized that there were many other people who would be more than willing to do so.

"Sabby, you gotta come with us," Anna repeated. "Ya just gotta." Anna tugged at Sabrina's arm, while Sabrina, embarrassed at Anna's excluding Francisco from the conversation, looked over at him apologetically.

"We'll talk about it later, Anna," Sabrina replied firmly. "Francisco and I came to take you out to dinner with us. I already arranged it with Mrs. Regan. Is she inside? I want her to meet Francisco."

The expectation of eating out with her sister, even if it did include 'Cisco, softened Anna a little. "OK," she said. "I'll go find Mrs. Regan."

Joanne greeted Francisco warmly as they entered the house, and they quickly fell into easy conversation about Sabrina, Anna, the group home, and a quickly found mutual shared interest -- big band music from the 1940's. As Francisco and Joanne chatted about Vaughn Monroe and other favorites, Sabrina took Anna aside. If things were to go any further between herself and Francisco, she wanted Anna to be comfortable with it.

"Why don't you want to be friendly with Francisco?" Sabrina asked her sister, with perhaps a little more irritation in her voice than she meant to convey.

"Mommy said bad things about him," Anna answered truthfully. "She didn't like him, so I don't either."

Sabrina sighed softly. "Anna, Mommy was trying to protect me, just the same as she always wanted to protect you. But she was wrong about Francisco. He's a very good person, and I love him. I really want you to be polite to him. Can you do that for me?" Still doubting that 'Cisco was worthy of her sister, but wanting to make Sabrina happy, Anna slowly nodded her head.

Meanwhile, during his conversation with Joanne, Francisco learned that the group home needed only $385 to make the residents' dream of a trip to Florida come true. He arranged to cover the remaining cost himself, making sure, however, that neither Sabrina nor Anna would learn where the final money had come from. Although initially surprised because most people wanted to be lauded for their magnanimity, Joanne agreed to keep his donation anonymous as she thankfully knew that the residents could now proceed with finalizing arrangements for their trip.

For dinner, Sabrina, Anna and Francisco went to Seventy Flavors, the restaurant where Anna now worked on an almost full time basis. Together, the three of them enjoyed munching on hot dogs and fries, and Anna proudly introduced her manager. They talked about matters of interest to Anna, including the Browns, swimming lessons offered free at the YMCA to Anna and her fellow group home residents, and planting flowers around the border of Anna's house. After overstuffing themselves, Sabrina refused the manager's offer of free ice cream, which brought another momentary pout from Anna. The pout was quickly replaced by an Anna-sized smile, however, when Francisco suggested that they go over to the mall to see if the latest Disney movie were still playing. Sabrina found her heart touched as Francisco showed over and over that he wanted to win Anna's affection. The visit which had begun so tenuously ended successfully when Anna gave Francisco an enormous hug when they finally returned her to her residence.

Driving home, Sabrina and Francisco tentatively began to talk about longer term planning for themselves, since Francisco would be leaving in less than two days.

"Beloved," Francisco said forthrightly, "I will make my home anywhere you want. I understand that you are selling your house here and moving into Cleveland. I can buy a house nearby, or we can live together in your house if you want. Or I will just rent somewhere and we will see each other as often as you like. Whatever you want, I am ready to do it. But this time, nothing must separate us."

With a pleading in her voice, Sabrina responded. "Dearest Francisco," she said tentatively, "I have been living alone for only a few years now. After being married for more than thirty-five years, I must tell you that I cherish being able to live on my own time schedule. The possibility of our being able to re-enter each others' worlds is only a couple of weeks old for me. It's too soon, at least for me, to be able to comprehend what has miraculously happened. I'm sorry, but I'm not yet ready to make long term commitments. When we're together, I can't imagine our ever being apart again. But when I let myself consider how different our lives are now, compared with forty years ago, I become terrified that we might make a huge mistake and turn the beauty of the past into a nightmare for the future." She paused. "I love you, Francisco. That has never wavered. I want to continue to be near you so we can learn if we can translate our wonderful past into the same kind of a future. But right now, I'm not ready to make irrevocable promises."

"Francisco blinked back tears. "I know, my love. I too am terrified, not of a future together, for which I have no doubts, but that we will not hold on to each other long enough to know. Please promise me that you will not make any decisions that might affect us both without first sharing your thoughts with me."

"That I can promise with no hesitation," Sabrina answered spontaneously. "I now understand how wrong I was to act without consulting you all those years ago," Sabrina continued. "But today I am hopefully more mature. Francisco del Oro, I promise to include you in any decisions that affect our futures."

"That's all I ask, Beloved, just that we make our choices together from now on."

FOURTEEN

The next two days disappeared into a blur. Sabrina took Francisco to see her condo in Cleveland. Because it was still under construction, however, she could only make an attempt at describing how it would look when construction was completed. Francisco admired the model the contractor took the time to show them while Sabrina explained that hers would look a little different because the lot she had chosen provided her more window space to view the park behind her new home.

In their brief time together, Sabrina tried hard to expose Francisco to everything impacting her current lifestyle. He was impressed that she worked out at a gym two or three times a week, listened as she described books she had read in the past month, and was astonished to learn that she had found a company on the internet where she could buy university level lectures. For a very small cost, Sabrina was now pursuing topics she had never had time to study during her undergraduate years.

"I'm learning about geology, Byzantine history, human physiology, anything I want," Sabrina announced as she proudly pointed to bookshelves filled with DVD's on an enormous variety of topics. "All I have to do is sit here and flip on the DVD player. Each lecture is half an hour, and I can replay any part as often as I want. It's wonderful." Sabrina's excitement exuded from her, and Francisco remembered how greatly he had always admired Sabrina's voracious love of learning.

When it was time to take Francisco to the airport, Sabrina felt as if she were losing a part of herself again. Just as miraculously as Francisco had suddenly reappeared into her life, now he was devastatingly gone. Although they agreed to stay in touch daily by either telephone or e-mail, Francisco explained that he would not be able to return to the States until February because of family obligations and an upcoming cataract surgery for himself. To Sabrina, February felt like eons away. By then her home on the lake would be sold and she would be living in a condo.

Suddenly, Sabrina laughed at herself. After forty years of not knowing what was happening in Francisco's life at all, what were a few more months? After only one hour of his being gone, she missed him dreadfully, but it was a different kind of feeling. No longer was she forced to accept that Francisco, her soul mate, the yin of her yang, the essence of her being, was erased from her life forever. That reality had once pulled her down to the depths of despair. Now she only had to count days until they would be together again. The truth of that seemed too bright to comprehend.

Between now and mid-February, a matter of only four months, Sabrina realized she had to pull herself together and answer some very hard questions. The way she normally made decisions, especially the tough ones, was to let the issue bubble in the back of her mind. She would not directly confront it until the time felt right. Sabrina did not consider this evading, just allowing things sort themselves out. When it was time, her mind would say 'okay, now start processing what I am sending up and figure out what to do about it'. She believed that method had worked well for her in the past, and she expected it to now.

Now when she went back to the attic to finalize her work, it seemed much easier. She was no longer so afraid of what she might find, although she knew there might still be a few ghosts hidden up there. Little by little, however, she found that there were none. Another box of childhood treasures was put on the donation pile without hesitation. Books were sorted through, and only the ones that still had relevance to her life went downstairs to her own bookcase. With many trips to the dump and even more to Goodwill, the Salvation Army and local charities, the attic floor eventually became bare.

Three days after Francisco left, Sabrina declared victory. Now it was time to call the auctioneer and discuss selling what had not been donated. First, though, Sabrina decided she deserved half an hour at the gym pool, which was her favorite form of exercise. She didn't mind working with the weights, but definitely preferred swimming laps. Finding her favorite swimsuit and throwing her hair dryer and towel into a bag, she drove off to what she happily designated 'Sabrina time'.

Twenty-two laps later, she lay in a lounge chair praising herself for being such a good girl. You've done your housework for the day, and you've also gotten good exercise, she preened. Now you deserve half an hour of unadulterated nothing. She closed her eyes and gradually sank into a peaceful sleep.

"Well, Sabrina. Fancy seeing you here."

Sabrina jumped as her eyes flew open and she reoriented herself to the poolside. Eventually she saw who had awakened her and felt greatly annoyed. Kenny, an old high school classmate, who she had heard was now divorced and on the prowl for any short term relationship, was grinning down at her.

"Did I startle you? Guess you were out in never, never

land, huh?" He smiled that false smile that had always set Sabrina's teeth on edge back in high school.

"Hi, Kenny. You take the day off from your office?" she asked as she sat up and draped the towel over her legs.

"Of course not. I'm prospecting for new customers here at the pool. Never know where you're gonna find someone looking to make a good solid investment." He chuckled at his own lame humor. "How about you? Haven't seen you here for a long time."

"That's right."

After a moment he realized that he was not going to get any more explanation. "How about running over to Burger King after we leave here and maybe make plans to go out sometime?" He made it sound as if he were offering her the chance of a lifetime.

"Actually, I'm not planning to leave soon. I have more laps to do, and then I may even go a round or two on the equipment circuit. I'll probably be a couple more hours or so. Maybe some other time."

Kenny got the message, although he clearly didn't like being put off. He flashed Sabrina another one of his false grins and hauled himself off to do more prospecting elsewhere. Sabrina was highly irritated as she settled back into her lounge chair, afraid that falling back asleep was now out of the question. She scanned the pool to see if there were anyone else she knew, but it was mid afternoon and the place was deserted except for one woman splashing around in the shallow end. The music, however, was comforting. At the moment they were playing classical selections, and Sabrina recognized Mozart's French Horn concerto, one of her favorites. With her eyes closed, she allowed herself to feel the crescendos and again began to relax.

Half an hour late, she forced herself out of the lounge chair and headed for the steam room, where she enjoyed inhaling the invigorating smell of eucalyptus. Most people complained about the aroma, saying that it smelled like Vicks, but Sabrina found it refreshing. After sitting there for ten minutes, she went out and boldly jumped directly into the ice plunge, emitting a yelp as the cold water closed her pores, and momentarily, her mind. She climbed out and decided to pass on the whirlpool today. She also decided to forego the circuit training as she headed for the showers and finally on home.

There were two messages awaiting her, one from a telemarketer and the other from Sally, with an invitation to stop over for dinner at seven o'clock. "Your choice, Chinese or pizza, either one delivered," Sally promised. That sounded better than eating alone tonight, Sabrina quickly decided, grateful for the diversion.

When she arrived, they opted for Thai food, enjoying

an enormous shared order of Pad Thai, followed by coconut ice cream. After cleaning up, the two of them curled up in Sally's wonderfully relaxing family room, each in a comfy overstuffed chair. After a bit of small talk, Sabrina cleared her throat and announced, "I have some hard decisions to make, and need your input to make sure I'm factoring in all the right data."

"Hmmm. Sounds like a computer equation to me, but go ahead. I'm listening," Sally replied humorously.

Sabrina too laughed at her poor choice of wording. "Francisco is coming back to the States in February," she started. "By then, I have to know whether or not I can marry him, and there's so much to take into consideration."

"No, you don't have to decide about anything as big as marriage," Sally interrupted. "You just need to decide if you want to continue any kind of relationship at all. If so, then how it will end up will become apparent in its own time. There are two people involved here, don't forget," she warned Sabrina. "Your decision making should not be a solo effort."

Sabrina sat upright, startled. Indeed, Francisco had stated emphatically that he wanted to provide input into any conclusion Sabrina reached, and here she was about to run off and make choices for the both of them, all on her own again.

Slowly, she nodded her head. "How right you are. I

need to work out what my options are, but I can't declare any absolutes. Wow, thanks. I'm already feeling more relaxed. Man, that's a lot easier on the mind," she said appreciatively.

Sabrina's major concern was the impact re-marriage would have on Anna, Paul and Karenna. She worried that her children would feel Sabrina was abandoning their father's memory, and that Anna would feel she was being pushed aside.

"Regarding Paul and Karenna," Sally observed wisely, "believe it or not, your children want you to be happy. Perhaps you can show them how to do that. Your example of following your heart might be exactly what they need to see."

"But they've never heard of Francisco," Sabrina responded, "other than knowing that I had a boyfriend in college. They're going to wonder how I just met someone and now want to contemplate a long term relationship."

"So, tell them," Sally replied in exasperation. "Explain that Francisco is not just any boyfriend from the past, but someone you have kept in your heart all these years. However," she warned, don't let them think their father was just a second best option for you. Tell them very clearly that you loved Frank for the man he was."

Sabrina accepted this advice with gratitude. Somehow, when someone else laid out the right way to do things, it was so much clearer that when you tried to figure it all out yourself, she acknowledged. Finally, Sabrina realized, she had learned that trusting someone else's judgment required a lot of courage, but that doing so sometimes resulted in seeing options more clearly and making better decisions.

"But what about Anna," Sabrina asked hesitantly. "I don't want to upset her world."

"Nonsense," Sally answered strongly. "Anna does not live with you. Indeed, you are about to move even further away from her than you are now, and she isn't upset about that. You will always be a part of Anna's life, but not necessarily the center of it. She can function just fine if she sees you once a week, or twice. Besides, she really likes Francisco now. She'll be happy for you, not upset."

Again, Sabrina felt some of the tension she had been accumulating begin to dissipate. She had always felt so afraid of letting people down, whereas what she was really doing, perhaps, was attaching too great an importance to her own role in other people's lives. She began to wonder if she forced herself into situations just to make herself feel valuable. "Thank you so much for being brave enough to pull me up by the short hairs when I need it. That is what a friend does, and I genuinely appreciate your wisdom and strength."

Sally quipped, "Just remember Sally's three 'R's. Rest,

right-mindedness and resolution. That will solve all the world's problems, and bring about universal peace."

"Okay," Sabrina answered back, "if I start with rest, I better get myself home and get some. I'll give you a call later in the week to bring you up to date on my right-mindedness. The resolution, well, we'll see about that."

FIFTEEN

The following morning, Sabrina called the auctioneer, asking him to assess her offerings and recommend what she should get further appraised. After that, she was feeling a bit restless and slowly strolled through her backyard down to the shoreline behind her house. As she approached the lake, she saw Tom coming out of his house. Sabrina waved, but did not go back to say hello. Just then she felt a need to be alone, to gaze at the lake and seek the solace it had provided her whenever she needed it most. As she walked out on the now decaying dock her father had built so many years ago, Sabrina savored the cool mid-October wind as it caressed her face. For a long while, she lost herself in reverie, then eventually walked back toward the house, stumbling over a tree root on the way. However, when she looked, she did not see anything sticking up above the ground that would have caused the misstep. Shrugging, she stopped over to see what Tom was puttering with.

"She needs another flower bed, my wife does," Tom muttered. "Just look at all these flower beds, all over the danged place. But no, she needs another one." Tom banged together some pieces of scrap wood while he continued to pretend to sulk. "Now just what does she think she wants to do, win another national prize, at her age?"

Sabrina chuckled, assured Tom that Martha could win prizes at any age, then heard her own phone ringing. Rushing in to answer it, Sabrina was disappointed to find that it was the group home director, asking if Sabrina could accompany the residents to Florida. He explained that the scheduled person had come down with shingles that morning, and it looked as if the trip might be cancelled if they could not find a replacement.

Sabrina recommended a very patient friend of hers who she knew would be delighted with a free trip to Disney World. After apologizing that she could not help out, she then spent the rest of the morning boxing items for the move to Cleveland. By two o'clock, she was ready for the auctioneer.

He arrived on time, accompanied by a young assistant who looked as if she were just learning the business. Taking his time to look carefully through Sabrina's designated items, the auctioneer recommended appraisals for some old books, several pieces of jewelry and some antique furniture that he thought might bring high bids if they had a current evaluation.

He suggested an auction date for early December, saying that would attract a lot of people looking for special holiday gifts.

As she listened to the auctioneer explain how to assess various items to his assistant, Sabrina found herself gaining confidence in his professionalism. Although she hated parting with these cherished items, she began to feel that someone else would come to love them as she had, and that revelation made her feel much better.

After the auctioneers left, however, Sabrina began to feel an overwhelming sadness. She wanted to cry but fought against it, until she finally realized how badly she needed to let down. Despondently, she allowed herself to ponder the many losses from her life. First, her belief in a safe and controllable world had been ripped from her in one brutal night, so many years ago. That loss had caused her to run from the cocoon of family and even love, and flounder perilously for years. Her capacity to trust had been yanked away like a torn fingernail, leaving only a throbbing pain that never covered itself properly again, although a facade had grown back.

Then she had lost not only her parents but also her husband and her youngest child. Her parents, yes, that was the way the world worked. Even losing Frank was to be expected at some point, although his being only in his late fifties seemed an atrociously early age to be taken away from her. But Sarah -- how could she ever reconcile herself to that? Sarah was a beautiful young woman, just starting her journey through life, and that death was something Sabrina could never accept. It just wasn't right, not fair, not just.

And in a sense, she had also lost her son and other daughter, although Sabrina still could not fathom where they had gone, or why. This, however, was a salvageable loss, she believed. Somehow, sometime, she could reconnect with them.

Now the contents of her childhood home were about to be auctioned off and the house sold. Although Sabrina had initiated the sale and knew it was the wisest course to take at this juncture in her life, it was still a terribly difficult separation. At last, Sabrina allowed herself to cry as she had not in decades, sobbing and moaning and acknowledging her grief until she felt totally consumed.

Eventually, Sabrina picked her head up to find herself draped across her bed, disheveled, weak, still shaking. She wished momentarily that she had a maid to bring her a cup of tea and a warm washcloth, then smiled wryly at herself. *Here you are, a fifty-nine year old woman, thinking you need someone to take care of you. You are still living, you have your health, your wealth and your relationships. Be thankful for that, and stop pitying yourself for what is lost.*

Those thoughts gave her the strength to force herself to sit up and make a deal. The deal was not with anyone else, but only with herself. She would take the advice she had learned from friends who had attended Alcoholics Anonymous. She would take one day at a time. Sometimes, she acknowledged, that's all you can do, and it's all you need to do.

Pulling herself off the bed, Sabrina went to the telephone and called her neurologist for a follow up appointment. She had seen him just before going to Atlantic City, and he said something about wanting to run some tests to find out why she stumbled rather frequently these days. In the whirlwind of the past couple of weeks, she had forgotten all about it, but this morning had reminded her.

Two days later, Sabrina arrived at the doctor's office a bit early and fell into conversation with another patient. This man, whom Sabrina judged to be in his forties, smiled at her as if from some inner happiness. Sabrina found the calmness he radiated refreshing. He spoke with great confidence about a positive future for mankind, and Sabrina was transported back to Vincennes, sitting in the park and talking with the young woman who had impressed her so greatly.

"I once knew someone," she said, "a teenage girl who exuded the same spirit of calmness and peace as you have. Where does it come from?"

"There's a prayer I say everyday," he answered, happy to share the source of his contentment. "It gives thanks to

God for creating me to know Him and to worship Him." He paused, then added, "You know, don't you, that God asks us to worship Him not because he needs our adulation, which He certainly does not, but to open our hearts so that His love will have a channel through which to travel to us. God communicates with us through our hearts, but we have to provide the pathway."

With considerable respect, Sabrina nodded, contemplating what he had said.

"Here, let me teach you this short saying. When Sabrina nodded again, he said, "Repeat after me. 'O Son of Being. Love Me, that I may love thee. If thou lovest me not, My love can in no wise reach thee'.

Sabrina repeated it once, then twice more. It was so short, but so full of meaning. "Where did you learn that?" she asked.

"I'm Baha'i," he answered, and Sabrina immediately recognized the name of the faith her young friend in Vincennes had espoused. "Yes, that's a religion I heard about years ago."

"If you'd like to learn more, we have a meeting every Wednesday night. I'll give you the address."

Sabrina happily accepted, remembering the feeling of strong fellowship and genuine peacefulness she had found so many decades before, and wondering if she might find it again. It briefly crossed her mind that if she had not married Frank and gotten so caught up in his world, perhaps she would have followed through with learning more about this faith. When the nurse called her new friend, he smiled again and said, "Hope to see you Wednesday." He was gone from the waiting room before she realized she had not asked his name. As she awaited her own appointment, Sabrina hoped that someday she might have that air of confidence, and she practiced the saying he had taught her.

A few minutes later when she was in In the doctor's examining room, the neurologist asked her to perform some movements, checked her responses and tested her strength, all the while chatting as if she were a long time friend. "Bruce tells me he taught you one of the sayings from the Hidden Words," he said. When Sabrina looked at him uncomprehendingly, he clarified. "Bruce, the man you were talking with in the waiting room."

"Oh," Sabrina said, wondering why the doctor would care about waiting room conversations.

"I'm Baha'i, too" the doctor explained. "Bruce has been my patient for a long time."

Sabrina was amazed, first to meet two people in one day who took her back to Vincennes, and second to learn that her physician believed in God.

"Doctors don't believe in a higher being," she blurted. "They think they are themselves God."

He laughed, so completely that Sabrina herself had to join in. "Oh, not all of us," he finally managed to say.

Following the exam, he told Sabrina that her stumbling was probably due to deteriorating muscle tone, despite her regular exercising. He recommended that she find a yoga class for people over the age of fifty, and told her that he wanted to see her again in four months. He explained that he did not want to put her on medication until he saw what progress she made with non medication treatment. Sabrina was grateful that he was not a pill pusher, and promised to look into the yoga. Just as she was getting off the examining table, however, she realized that she would be living somewhere else in four months.

"I won't be here," she said. "I'm moving into Cleveland."

"That's not far," the neurologist responded. You could come back. If you prefer, though, I'll give you the names of some doctors nearer where you live. You can decide later."

As she was driving home, Sabrina recalled a philosophy that a supervisor from her first job had once explained. That woman, who was highly regarded not only by employees but by management as well, had said that there were three things that we humans had to do every day to maintain a happy lifestyle. It had been so many years, but Sabrina was pleased to realize that, after she thought about it for a moment, she remembered all three lessons.

First, the supervisor had said, people had to take care of themselves physically. This meant eating right, getting enough rest, and, very important, exercising adequately so the body could manage to cope with daily demands. When a frazzled co-worker complained that she never had time to exercise, the supervisor gently reminded that young mother that if she didn't take care of herself, she would eventually not be taking very good care of anyone else. The supervisor went on to say that someone who was too tired, too poorly nourished or not in good physical condition behaved badly toward others, made excuses for not participating in important family events and eventually began to fail to take good care of the emotional needs of those they loved. A lot of people who heard her had nodded in agreement, recognizing patterns from their own lives.

Second, the sage woman continued, it is essential that we learn something new every day. It could be from a formal setting such as a classroom, or from listening to a talk show that offered varying opinions, or even making a daily effort to study something of particular interest. Whether we like it or not, she had said, life changes. Without ongoing learning, stagnation takes over and people become complacent, which ultimately leads to poor decision-making. Refusing to equip ourselves with a better comprehension of the world around us is a direct path to misery, she had warned.

Finally, the third part of happiness was the most crucial, the supervisor had stated simply but with utter conviction. Everyone has to seek his or hew own understanding of the spiritual world. She had then gone on to recommend that by studying writings from many religions, people could better understand their own faith.

This pronouncement had again startled Sabrina. Although as a child, Sabrina had attended church every week, she had never been encouraged to think closely about the teachings she was exposed to, and certainly not to doubt the truth of what the minister said. Her part in religion, she had been taught as a child, was to repeat prayers and sing songs, not challenge teachings. She had been brought up to believe that the clergy was trained to understand the word of God, and it was the responsibility of the congregation to look to their minister for spiritual knowledge and guidance. Study of other faiths had certainly never been encouraged.

As she thought about these long forgotten thoughts from someone she had once greatly admired, Sabrina realized that the spiritual part was the one piece of fulfillment she had neglected. She had always taken good care of herself physically. She had stayed current on world events, had fun in book clubs and social groups, and in general maintained a solid intellectual curiosity. However, she had not pursued the spiritual side of her being, which resulted in her children being brought up without religious training. It occurred to Sabrina that this might be why they seemed so ungrounded today. Perhaps, if life were indeed a three legged stool, she had not given her children or herself that third leg -- spirituality -- to provide stability to their every day lives.

Sabrina pulled into her driveway and sat in the car for a moment, considering this new thought. Yes, she would go to the fireside Wednesday to see if she could begin working on the spiritual deficit of her life. What could it hurt?

Meade Saeedi

SIXTEEN

To her surprise, it was only a few days later when the realtor brought Sabrina an acceptable offer. She was greatly relieved that even though settlement would occur at the end of December, the buyers had agreed that she could remain in the house and pay rent until mid January when her new home would be ready.

For her new location, Sabrina had selected a recently constructed community on the west side of Cleveland. Most people buying there were in their twenties and thirties, and the broker was surprised when a woman of Sabrina's age indicated interest in the that area. Sabrina assured him that she enjoyed being around young people, and had no concerns about fitting comfortably into these new surroundings. Sabrina's real worry had been that living in a condo rather than a single family home would be too great a change in her lifestyle, since she was accustomed to having a lot of private outdoor space for her personal enjoyment. Fearing that having to take an elevator to her front door would become intolerable, Sabrina had carefully chosen a ground level setting with a large terrace behind the condo. There was seating for several people on the terrace, plus space for an outdoor grill. One block behind her home was a park to which she could walk easily and safely, and this served perfectly to accommodate her need for outdoor space. With careful planning, Sabrina was pleased to find, change was not that difficult to cope with.

The following Wednesday night, Sabrina dressed carefully to attend the Baha'i fireside Bruce had invited her to. When she arrived, she was surprised to see people dressed casually, sitting comfortably in the hosts' living room and chatting animatedly with one another. *This is not like any church I've ever been to*, she thought.

Bruce introduced Sabrina to the hosts, a couple in their late twenties who had both been born into Baha'i families. "We're the exception," they told Sabrina. "Most people come to the Baha'i faith from other religions."

Bruce told Sabrina his story of growing up in a strong Catholic tradition. While in college, a roommate told him about a faith that encouraged individual thinking, and he had looked into it because the concept of investigation of the truth appealed to him. After a year he decided this was the faith he wanted to be affiliated with, and now, after thirty years, Bruce was still a dedicated Baha'i.

Half an hour later, the formal fireside began. After an invitation to offer prayers from any religion and language, during which Sabrina heard offerings in Spanish, Urdu and English, the host offered a brief introduction.

"Welcome, friends. I'm so pleased to see new faces as well as many who have been here before. This meeting is called a fireside because we sit around and talk like friends around a warm and comforting fire. Sometimes we discuss specific topics, and often we just address whatever issues people want to bring up. Tonight we are privileged to have a guest speaker, Linda Stone, who will be talking about the similarities found among all faiths. Baha'is call this concept 'progressive revelation', and I hope you find Linda to be a wealth of information for you."

For the next hour, Sabrina listened with fascination as Linda explained that Baha'is believe there is only one God who has sent messengers to humanity over time, in accordance with the capacity of different stages of civilization to comprehend the teachings delivered by each messenger. Linda began by talking about the Zoroastrians. Sabrina had never heard of this faith, and was shocked to learn that the Magi who had come from the East to worship the Christ child were Zoroastrian, a faith almost as old as Judaism. Why hadn't her childhood minister ever told the congregation who the Magi were, she wondered?

As the evening progressed, Sabrina listened to people from Protestant and Catholic backgrounds, an Israeli Jew, a Buddhist, and a couple people who described themselves as 'agnostics looking to be proved wrong' as they asked questions and explained the traditions and beliefs they had grown up with. Like Sabrina, they too were investigating what role they wanted religion to play in their lives, and Linda answered questions with courtesy as well as solid reasoning, which Sabrina found refreshing.

Sabrina wondered if Frank, from wherever he was, could follow her spiritual quest, and whether he too would have been interested in this faith if he had known about it during his lifetime. Sabrina was pretty sure he would have, since Baha'is did not condemn any previous religion, but instead emphasized that all faiths came from the same God, and that all humanity is equal in God's eyes. One teaching that really appealed to Sabrina was that no national or religious group was inferior to any other. As she considered this, she remembered how she had been castigated for dating someone from South America during her college days.

Bringing her mind back to the discussion, Sabrina nodded as she heard that only social teachings change from one revelation to another, but that spiritual teachings remain the same throughout all great religions. The monotheistic faiths

-- Zoroastrianism,   Buddhism, Judaism, Christianity, Islam -- all taught spiritual principles such as love of God, love of neighbor, social justice and upright conduct. Only teachings relating to social conventions like food restrictions or marriage laws changed from one revelation to the next. As she thought about it, she recalled hearing these same ideas from her friend in Vincennnes, but had since forgotten about them.

By the end of the evening, Sabrina was entranced with what she had learned. However, although she found the discussions stimulating, she had no expectation of ever becoming a Baha'i herself. Many years before, she had promised herself never to commit to anything with which she might later become disillusioned.

The following morning, Sabrina looked carefully at herself in the mirror. She was pleased to note that she did not see an almost sixty year old face looking back. Rather, she saw a face seeking much more to life than it had already experienced, and she wondered briefly what the future would hold for her. She felt sure that Francisco would be a part of that future, but was still not certain how. As she brushed her teeth, she was pleased that they were all still her own, and her complexion needed little makeup to look natural. Sabrina believed she was, overall, pretty content with her existence at this stage of her life. However, she fully realized that there was still more 'out there' to experience, and was grateful that she was not afraid to search even though she didn't have any concept of where those experiences might lead her.

Between the present and February, however, Sabrina realized that she had Thanksgiving and Christmas to endure, and she would probably be alone, except for Anna. Thanksgiving was only a couple of weeks away, and both Paul and Karenna had already told her they would not be coming to Ohio. Karenna told her mother stories of multiple obligations, and Paul informed her that he was about to finalize his third divorce and therefore planned to spend the holidays skiing in Vail. However, because of this last failed marriage, Paul now seemed to be slightly more amenable to having at least one positive relationship in his life, and he had promised his mother that he would come to visit her in the spring at her new home.

Two weeks later, for Thanksgiving dinner, Sabrina made a small turkey breast, prepared a special recipe for corn pudding, and added coleslaw and Harvard beets, all of which were Anna's favorite holiday foods. The two of them celebrated their final Thanksgiving in the house on the lake on Wednesday, since the group home was having its own big dinner on Thursday. Tom and Martha were happy to join them, and they contributed a baked Alaska, which they remembered as Anna's favorite dessert.

Over the next few weeks, Sabrina attended more firesides,

continuing to listen and beginning to participate, but still withholding herself from any commitment. On her third visit, Sabrina invited Sally to go with her. To Sabrina's astonishment, Sally embraced the faith immediately, declaring after two meetings that she wanted to become Baha'i. This flabbergasted Sabrina, but made sense to others there. Some people, she was told, instantly recognize God's latest message to mankind, while others need to spend more time searching their own hearts and thinking about the teachings. One woman explained that she had spent sixteen years attending Baha'i events before she realized this was the right faith for her. "Comprehension comes to everyone at the right time for that individual," she assured Sabrina.

On Christmas Eve, Sabrina took Anna out for barbecued ribs at Bob Evans, and Anna had proudly given her sister a ceramic Christmas tree that she had painted and decorated herself. "I didn't tell ya about it 'cause I really wanted it to be a surprise," Anna stated with such feeling that tears sprang to Sabrina's eyes.

"Oh, Antsy," she answered, "this took so much work. How did you get the bulbs to stay in? Did you have to glue them?"

"Yup, and sometimes they didn't fit right. But Mrs. Regan, she helped me. When you turn on the light inside, they look real pretty, don't they, huh?"

Anna was equally delighted with the $100 gift certificate to her favorite clothing store at the mall, accompanied by Sabrina's promise to take Anna shopping before the move to Cleveland.

On Christmas Day, Sally had gone out of town to be with her grandchildren, and Tom and Martha had two of their children visiting. Sabrina sat alone in her kitchen, wondering what the next holiday season would be like for her. Would Francisco be living nearby, or might they even be married? Would Paul and Karenna finally be sharing a holiday season with their mother? Would she have a new circle of friends? How would she adapt to these changes?

As Sabrina pondered these things, she became aware that somehow her perspective was changing. She was beginning to see the world from a point of view that was no longer just material and factual, but also had spiritual components. Decision making regarding how to deal with her life was no longer a black and white process, she found. Instead, Sabrina realized that allowing her thinking to be motivated by spiritual principles such as trustworthiness, reliability and integrity emboldened her to perceive the points of view of other people, not just to rely on her own experience. She gradually felt the beginnings of being able to trust other people's judgment, and not to be solely dependent on herself to chart her future. With that understanding, Sabrina was amazed to find that a little more of the tension that controlled her life so completely began to ease.

SEVENTEEN

By the end of the second week of January in the new millennium, Sabrina's move to a new life was over. She was settling nicely into her new condominium and enjoying the freedom to decorate this newly constructed home in any manner she chose. She smiled wryly as she recalled the horrendous disputes from previous moves, when Frank would want to take everything, while Sabrina would try to use moving day as an excuse to discard as much as she could. Indeed, for her new home Sabrina had brought only a few items from her past, including some heirloom china, a writing desk from France that she and Frank had purchased on one of their first trips abroad, and most of her books, as well as practical things like her cookware and everyday dishes. She had auctioned off the rest of the accumulated collection from the last thirty-five years of her life, after giving Paul and Karenna first dibs on whatever they wanted. They had both asked for a few things to be shipped to them, with which Sabrina had dutifully complied, noting that Paul wanted his grandfather's hand tools, and Karenna asked for the family silverplate.

Thus far, Sabrina had purchased only a few pieces of furniture, waiting for the right items to find her rather than rushing to fill empty space. Other than her small apartment in Vincennes, Sabrina reflected, she had never really had a free hand in molding her living space to fit her own tastes. Her mother's preferences had dominated her childhood bedroom, the college dorm was pretty standard with little opportunity for individuality, and Frank had insisted on bringing a lot of his family furnishings into all the homes where they had lived as a married couple. Now, as she looked around her new surroundings, Sabrina felt wonderfully liberated. Although she still had a lot of empty space, she appreciated that she could slowly choose only what truly called to her and nothing else.

Sabrina had met two of her new neighbors, both of whom had already invited her to visit their own homes. Although she found their styling choices beautiful, she did not think the homes were livable. Both women, one married and the other still single, had hired interior decorators to choose fabrics and recommend furniture, which Sabrina considered not only a frivolous waste of money, but also would need changing in a few years. *Just wait 'til they have kids*, she thought to herself with a laugh.

Being eclectic by nature, Sabrina did not follow any particular style, choosing instead whatever appealed to her innately. Each day since the move, she had gone out and browsed, sometimes coming back with a treasure, often returning empty handed.

Her first purchase had been a wonderfully comfortable space-age foam mattress into which she molded herself luxuriously each night. Then she found a headboard which was a light yellow padded fabric, shaped perfectly to be comfortable for reading herself to sleep at night. The saleswoman had told her that fabric was beginning to go out of style, but Sabrina didn't care. She liked the look and feel of it, and bought it on impulse.

In another store, she found the rest of her bedroom furniture. To give herself more space in this home, where the bedroom was considerably smaller than she was used to, she eliminated the footboard and the upholstered bench at the end of the bed. Spotting an ornately designed Middle Eastern trunk in a specialty shoppe, she bought it to enhance the corner under the window, leaving the trunk open and allowing her extra blankets to tumble out. The dresser she selected was designed from a beautiful pecan wood, with a matching nightstand that had a pull out shelf where she could put her book down at night. In yet another store, she chose a kitchen set consisting of a round ceramic top table that fit perfectly into the breakfast nook with three chairs having different colored padding on the seats, one each in yellow, blue and red. She also found a recliner for the living room, to remind herself of her father.

Returning home from one of her shopping trips, Sabrina looked outdoors at the gathering clouds and remembered that the weatherman had been predicting a major snow system for the past two days. If it did not come tomorrow, Sabrina had made plans to do some looking for knick knacks with Sally. She had always marveled at Sally's choices in home decorating, and trusted her friend's input into making her own home feel perfect. Also, she admitted to herself, she was beginning to get bored shopping by herself all the time.

Sabrina had not yet had a chance to go walking in the nearby park. However, she had transferred her fitness club membership to a facility only three blocks from her condo, and had already enjoyed their lap pool twice. She was delighted to be rid of nuisances like Kenny, although she readily acknowledged that there would probably be more like him at this club, too.

That night, Sabrina read herself to sleep, but was awakened in the pre-dawn hours by howling winds. At first, she just wanted to snuggle back under the goose down duvet on her new bed, but then decided to wrap the comforter around herself and sit in the recliner in front of the sliding glass door so she could watch the storm. She stopped in the kitchen to fix herself a cup of hot cocoa, then settled into the chair and closed her eyes for a moment so she could just listen to the wind. When she opened her eyes, she saw that the snow was now piled eight inches up the glass door. *Well, so what,* she thought with a smile. The snow could melt when it melted. The Homeowners Association was responsible to keep sidewalks and parking areas cleaned out, and she had nowhere urgent to go. She would probably have to cancel the shopping trip with Sally, but at least she no longer had to dig out a long driveway. Indeed, all Sabrina had to do now was walk out her front door, which was protected by a long overhang, and drive her car out of an already shoveled parking lot. *Ah, yes*, she thought cozily.

Watching the storm, Sabrina thought about each snow flake's being unique, and wondered how that could be with so many of them out there. Eventually she decided that it did not matter whether or not she understood each and every mystery in life. She no longer felt that she had to be in complete and total control of everything all the time. Indeed, it was okay to allow others to lead sometimes, she considered drowsily. With that thought in her head, she fell asleep and awoke very well rested a few hours later.

She stretched and gradually unfolded herself from the recliner. As she glanced outside and saw that the snow was now more than a foot deep, she pondered what to do for the day. No shopping, no shoveling, no nothing today, she decided. Instead, this was the day she would light her first fire in the fireplace.

Making herself a bowl of oatmeal, she sliced in a banana and poured on some skim milk. The phone rang with an offer of a free two day trip to Florida if she would spend forty-five minutes listening to an offer for a wonderful alternative living opportunity. Although it sounded tempting as she watched the blizzard outside, Sabrina answered confidently that she was not interested. Then, for a moment after the call, she wondered how it had come through since she was on both the state and national lists guaranteeing no soliciting telephone calls. Realizing that she had a new telephone number, she wrote herself a note to notify the no-call authorities to add the new Cleveland number to their list.

Knowing that she was not going anywhere that day, she spent the morning tidying up and making a list of stores to visit with Sally when the blizzard died out. She even called the home delivery grocery store and ordered fruits, salad makings and a steak. At the last second, she added a homemade pecan pie, which she justified by promising herself to invite her neighbors over later that afternoon when she lit the fire.

She was still in her flannel pajamas an hour later when she returned to the recliner with the latest bestseller. She read for a while, but soon found herself getting restless. She got up and paced, then sat at the kitchen table. She hated this feeling of confinement, and wondered briefly if maybe she should spend her retirement days in a warm climate where she could get outside whenever she wanted. Nonsense, she chided herself, this was only going to last for a couple of days. In warm places there were hurricanes and insects, and other things that interfered with going outside, too. Watching the storm was pleasant, she was safe and warm, she did not have to go to work, and she had plenty of food. She mused that it was much too easy to slip into complaining and reminded herself how much more effective it was to add up all the things that were right.

Feeling better, she began to think about what activities she could plan for when Francisco arrived, which was now less than two weeks away. Maybe they could take a trip to Cedar Point, the amusement park in western Ohio. Anna would love to go with them, Sabrina knew. Just for herself and Francisco, she would get tickets to the Cleveland Symphony and maybe a Cavaliers game. Perhaps she would take him to a fireside, if he were interested. She allowed herself to revel in the feelings of intense happiness invoked by thinking about Francisco as she prepared for her afternoon guests. Then the telephone rang again, interrupting Sabrina's mental sojourn into ecstasy. When she answered, she was amazed to hear Karenna asking,

"Hello, Mother. How are you?"

Sabrina's immediate reaction was that there had been some sort of catastrophe. Although Sabrina had called both her children to let them know her new address and phone number, she had been in Cleveland for nearly three weeks, this was Karenna's first call to her mother since the move. Sabrina's maternal instincts prepared her for possible danger, and she therefore spoke soothingly to mask her surprise.

"Hello, Karenna. It's so wonderful to hear your voice." Forcing herself to laugh, she added, "We're having quite a snowstorm here, and I'm starting to get cabin fever. So how's everything with you guys? Is John okay?"

In a tone that sounded almost friendly, Karenna responded, "We're both fine," and Sabrina's anxiety melted. Then Karenna added, "Actually, John and I are coming to Cleveland on a business trip next week, and I was hoping you might have some time to spend with me."

Recovering from the astonishment she felt, Sabrina answered, "Of course, Karenna. I'm thrilled you're coming. Tell me which airline and I'll meet you there."

"It's next Wednesday, and we arrive at 11:15 in the morning, on Southwest," Karenna replied. "If you have your cell phone with you, I'll call when we get to the curb line, so you don't have to pay for parking."

Was this Karenna, thinking about her mother's convenience? Sabrina couldn't quite believe it.

Karenna continued. "John has an early afternoon meeting, so I can spend the day with you, if that's all right."

"That's perfect, Karenna." Sabrina wanted to say 'Darling' instead of 'Karenna', but decided not to push her luck. "I'm looking forward to seeing you so much."

"Actually, I am too, Mother," came the answer. "I have a lot of things to talk about with you."

After hanging up, Sabrina wondered if Karenna were pregnant and had decided to mend relations for that reason. Whatever the cause, Sabrina floated on cloud nine for the rest of the day.

The delivery groceries arrived, and Sabrina had invited her neighbors to come over at four o'clock. Although surprised by the invitation, both young women immediately accepted, and the three of them enjoyed an hour of chatting about such varied topics as music, current best sellers, horseshows and local politics. The women raved about the pecan pie as they gave Sabrina their thoughts about what style sofas she should get. When they left, Sabrina had a comfortable feeling that she had just begun some new friendships, which pleased her greatly.

Wanting to capitalize on her success, Sabrina decided to

chance calling Paul. Not knowing whether she would get surliness or a friendly chat, she nervously dialed the number. To her surprise, Paul answered on the third ring.

"Hello, Son," she greeted warmly. "Do you have a minute to talk?"

"Is something wrong? Is Karenna okay?" Paul immediately leapt to the worst conclusions, as usual, then Sabrina realized she had done the same thing when Karenna called.

"No, no. Everything's fine. We're having a blizzard here, and it reminded me of some storms we endured back in Chicago. Do you remember any of those?"

"I remember when you and Dad were late coming home one night," Paul answered bitterly, "and the babysitter told us that so many people had been hurt in car accidents that night, she doubted you would be coming home at all."

"Oh, my God," a horrified Sabrina stammered. "I never knew about that. I am so sorry, Paul. You must have been terrified. Which babysitter was it? If I had known, I never would have entrusted you to her again."

"It's okay, Mom. Just one of those things that happen to kids. You guys came home a few hours later, so we knew it was a lie," Paul answered, trying now to soothe his mother. "Anyway, I'm getting along pretty well now. I finally have to take care of myself, and I'm getting better at it." He paused, then went on,"You won't believe this, but I've started to see a therapist. I'm actually beginning to take responsibility for my own behavior instead of blaming my wife or co-worker or anyone else in my path for whatever goes wrong in my life."

At this, Sabrina sat down hard on the kitchen chair. "Paul, I am *so* proud of you. I know how difficult a decision that must have been. If the therapist ever wants to talk with me, I'll be glad to see him."

"Actually, it's a her," Paul said, "and I don't think she wants to involve family members just yet. But I'll mention it and see what she thinks. Thanks for the offer."

Sabrina knew that this was a cut off for that topic. However, they chatted for another fifteen minutes and when Paul said good bye, he thanked his mother for calling in what sounded like a very heartfelt manner.

Sabrina shook her head unbelievingly as she hung up. She knew that nothing had yet been resolved, but she felt very positive that improved communications with her son were starting. And it looked as if there might be a thawing with Karenna, as well. Whatever was causing these changes, Sabrina was very grateful. *Thank you God, whatever you are.*

EIGHTEEN

On Wednesday morning, Sabrina parked in the short-term lot, despite Karenna's offer to meet her outside on the curb. She was now awaiting the latest update on the flight from Dallas, which was already an hour late because of delays caused by thunderstorms.

The airline representative smiled reassuringly at the anxious mother who said she was meeting her pregnant daughter, saying, "The plane was diverted around a heavy weather system, Ma'am, so it's taking longer to arrive. It should be here in another eighteen minutes." The specificity of eighteen minutes helped relieve Sabrina's anxiety, and she knew that landing conditions in Cleveland were good that morning. Nonetheless, she hated having her reunion with Karenna delayed by even one more second, so continued to pace. Eventually, she sat down and determined to settle herself. Sabrina had not seen her daughter since the night of Karenna's wedding, now more than five years past. What if Sabrina blew it today? What if she said something that upset Karenna rather than helped ease their largely shredded relationship?

It was too late for terror. The delayed flight was at the gate, and here came Karenna and John. Sabrina took a deep breath and hoped for the best. She allowed Karenna to set the tone, receiving a nice hug from her daughter and a jolly 'hi' from her son-in-law. Because John was being met by someone from his company, the women agreed to meet him for dinner at seven o'clock. Sabrina recommended the restaurant, and John answered that he had heard good things about the seafood there.

Now that they were alone, Sabrina took the first plunge. "My car is in short-term parking," Sabrina said as an ice breaker. "Once we get it, would you like to stop somewhere for a ladies' lunch, or go back to my condo to eat? I have plenty of fixings for sandwiches."

"Is Le Chez Rouge anywhere near here?" Karenna asked. "Someone told me it a really chic place to eat. And it's my treat," she added.

"It's not far," Sabrina replied, "and I've been wanting to try it out, so that will be perfect." She could tell that Karenna was surprised that her mother even knew of the restaurant, and she silently thanked her new neighbors for putting her in the know.

Upon arrival, Karenna gave her name to the maitre d', who looked a bit miffed that they did not have reservations. Nonetheless, he directed them to a reasonably nice table in a quiet location.

"I'm having the Chez Rouge salad," Karenna announced after spending a longer time than necessary perusing the menu. "Mom, I think you might like the salmon."

This amused Sabrina, who had never in her life ordered fish in a restaurant while her children were growing up. Recently, however, she had been forcing herself to eat seafood a couple times a week for health reasons, and salmon happened to be her favorite type of fish. "I think you're right. I'll try that." Karenna looked at her with surprise, then gave their orders to the waiter.

After the server left, Sabrina waited for Karenna to bring up whatever it was that had brought her to Cleveland. "Mom," Karenna began tentatively, "I want to say something, and I'm sure it will surprise you. What I want to say is, well . . . I'm sorry we've become estranged." Karenna heaved a sigh of relief. "There, I got the words out," she said, looking embarrassed. "I know it's partly because of my own bad temper, even though I normally blame you for anything that goes wrong between us. What I'd like t say is, I'd like to make things better, if that's possible."

Sabrina did not answer her daughter, not because she did not have anything to say, but because her voice box would not produce sound. She looked down at her hands, then back up at Karenna. The tears in her eyes said far more than her words could ever convey. Finally, she made the simplest answer she could. "Thank you," she said.

Karenna gently reached over and took her mother's hands in her own. She enjoyed the feeling of being the strong one this time. "I know this is taking you by surprise, and we'll discuss it more later," Karenna soothed. "Right now, I need to tell you that I lost my first pregnancy a month ago. It was a spontaneous abortion, and even though the doctor explained it to me, I still don't understand how that can happen. Once you're pregnant, I always though you stayed that way until that baby was born, but I guess it doesn't always happen like that. John and I were devastated, but we're starting to adjust."

"Oh, Sweetheart, I'm so sorry." Sabrina started to reach over to hug Karenna, but her daughter flinched sway.

"It's okay," Karenna interjected to stop her mother's show of more public affection than she could tolerate. "We'll try again soon. Anyway, for right now, let's just chat about everyday things. Are you settled into your new home?"

Sabrina nodded her head, although it was not clear to Karenna whether this was an acknowledgement of her daughter's pain or an attempt to say yes to the question about the move.

Sabrina took a deep breath and answered the latter. "The move went better than I expected, both in terms of getting all the household stuff to the condo in one piece, and getting me to the condo in one piece." Although Sabrina laughed, it was with a brittleness that tore at her inside. "I thought it was going to be really terrible to leave my childhood home, and it was. But ultimately I was able to let go and be free, and now I'm very comfortable with what I did. I like my new home and my neighbors, plus I'm having the time of my life decorating exactly the way I want."

"What kind of furniture are you selecting?" Karenna asked. "I bet it's a little bit of everything, rather than according to any particular style. Am I right?"

"Absolutely," Sabrina agreed. "Perhaps, if you have time today, you and I could stop at this one store where there are two pieces I'm trying to decide between. I would really appreciate your input."

"I'd love to do that. Thanks for asking me," came the thankful reply

When their food arrived, Karenna spoke a little more about suffering a miscarriage and how that had set her to thinking about the difficulties of being a parent, of making choices that a child might or might not like, but always having to do what was right for the child. "It took me a long time to realize that being a parent is not the same as being a buddy," Karenna confessed.

They discussed that concept throughout most of the meal, then Karenna changed the subject. "Paul called me a while ago. He's separated from number three, which is a blessing, so far as I am concerned. She was a tartlet, if ever I saw one. Paul needs someone a lot more stable, and I for one am grateful that she's finally out of the picture."

"Actually," Sabrina answered, "I spoke with Paul just a few days ago. He told me that he was on his own again, and that he's finally getting therapy. I hope he can recover some of his faith in the world. It is truly awful to go through life thinking that this is all there is, and being so disappointed with what happens day to day."

Karenna looked at her mother in amazement. "Mother, are you beginning to turn religious on me? You, who had no use for church, no use for a belief in, quote, false gods?"

Sabrina smiled at her daughter in a way that Karenna had never seen before. "Maybe it's old age creeping up on me," Sabrina answered. "Or maybe I had to find the right answers. But yes, I've come across a faith that makes sense, at least to me. I'll tell you whatever you want to know about it," Sabrina answered her daughter.

"This has got to be good!" was Karenna's unbelieving response. "Is it one of those Holy Roller things? Charismatic Christianity? You haven't gone Muslim, have you? What on earth has happened to your brain? You, of all people, turning to religion?"

"Wonders never cease," was Sabrina's calm response. "As I said, I'll tell you anything you want to know. Right now, though, let's go look at that furniture. I guess first we need to stop at my condo so you can see what's already there."

When Sabrina pulled into her development, Karenna was duly impressed. "This is where you live?" she asked incredulously. "I never thought you would want anything so modern looking."

"I probably seemed like an old fogey when I was your day-to-day mother," Sabrina responded humorously, "but really, I'm quite young at heart." She waved to a neighbor who looked Karenna's age and reminded her to come for lunch the following week. "I think you'll like the inside," she called over her shoulder to Karenna.

When they stepped inside the condo, Karenna was stunned. It looked like a movie set. There was an island covered with a granite counter top, built in bookcases, full length windows that overlooked a park setting, cathedral ceilings, recessed lighting, even a whirlpool tub. "Mom, this is magnificent!"

Karenna finally managed to get out. "You really chose this yourself? I guess I think of you as a seventies Mom, and this is just beyond belief to me."

"I'm on my own now," Sabrina answered. This time around, I get to choose everything, just the way I like it.

"Well, it's very tasteful," Karenna said approvingly. "You haven't bought much furniture yet, I see. Still looking for just the right things?"

"Yup, as I always told you not to say."

Karenna looked at her mother and burst into laughter, while the ice melted a little more. "Let me look around, so I have a feel for what will look good where." Karenna walked though the living room, two bedrooms, den, kitchen and dining area, then pronounced herself ready to go.

Sabrina and Karenna went out on a mother-daughter shopping trip together for the first time in decades. Together, they finally selected the tan microfiber couch and loveseat, agreeing that it enhanced the feeling of calmness in the living room. Sabrina had been considering purchasing a different style of loveseat, one with reclining chairs, but Karenna pointed out that that would be redundant, since there was already one recliner in the room. After a moment's consideration, Sabrina nodded and agreed.

Then Karenna spotted an end table and after looking it

over carefully, decreed that it would be perfect in the angle between the loveseat and the sofa. When Sabrina agreed, Karenna insisted on buying it as a housewarming present for her mother, while Sabrina pinched herself hard to be sure she was not lost in one of her daydreams.

After making arrangements with the store to deliver the furniture the following day, Sabrina and Karenna returned to Sabrina's condo. It was already 6:15 PM, so they had only forty-five minutes before they were to meet John for dinner. Sabrina promised that Karenna could soak in the jacuzzi on the next visit, and Karenna assured her mother that she would take her up on that.

They arrived at the restaurant simultaneously with John, who observed his wife carefully to assess how the afternoon had gone. He visibly relaxed when he saw a genuine smile of happiness on Karenna's face. During dinner, they briefly discussed John's afternoon with business associates, which had been quite boring. Eventually they moved on to the women's afternoon, and Karenna described her mother's new home in glowing terms. "It is both classically beautiful and wonderfully comfortable," Karenna gushed, while Sabrina listened in astonishment. "And we shopped for living room furniture this afternoon. Mom had narrowed it down to two excellent choices, and we ended up with the simpler style which matched the serenity of her living space." John noted that his wife had said 'we ended up' and glanced at Karenna with approval. For so many years, he had been trying to get his wife to make an effort to heal the anger that upset her so much of the time. Indeed, although Karenna had not admitted this to her mother, John was the prime motivation behind her contact, although Karenna's own newly developing understanding of the difficulty of being a parent had pushed her to say 'yes' when John suggested she accompany him on this business trip.

After dinner, Sabrina dropped them both off at their hotel, but only after extracting a promise that they would come back soon for a prolonged visit. When she returned home, she called Sally, who was ecstatic that the visit had gone so well. "It doesn't sound as if you talked much about the past, which is where the anger still is, and it will have to be dealt with eventually. Don't expect that everything is now perfect," Sally warned. "There will still be a lot of bumps in the road. But at least you two are talking again, and John's positive attitude will be invaluable. It sounds like Karenna found herself a real gem for a husband."

Sally relayed the latest goings on in the Baha'i community, where she was now an active member, then made arrangements to meet Sabrina when she came to visit Anna on Thursday. Sabrina mentioned her butterflies-in-the-stomach when she thought about Francisco's return, which was now less than a week away, and Sally soothed her for a while but eventually realized that nothing could really calm jitters based on such big issues as a future together or apart with the man Sabrina once loved, and apparently still did.

That night Sabrina curled up in front of her fireplace and began to read A Thief in the Night, one of the many books the Baha'is had given her. The author, William Sears, was a journalist who had decided to investigate the proclaimed return of Christ, which according to many biblical scholars had been expected sometime around the middle of the nineteenth century. Once she began reading, she became utterly fascinated with Sears' investigations, and it was well after two o'clock in the morning by the time her eyes finally closed.

Later in the morning, she kept an eye out for the furniture delivery truck while enjoying mini croissants from the local bakery, along with some almond tea and a pear. When the furniture arrived, Sabrina was shocked that it looked so much larger in her condo than it had in the showroom, but eventually she had it arranged in a manner that she liked.

With the weather clearing, Sabrina finally had a chance to go for a walk in the nearby park. She enjoyed the calls of the cardinals and bluejays, and laughed as she watched the squirrels arguing loudly over lunch options. Although the path had not yet been cleared, she had no difficulty trudging through the melting snow. *This really is lovely*, she thought. *Leaving my lake is not so difficult as I had anticipated. I guess there's beauty everywhere, and changing the scenery probably does me a lot of good.* She wandered for more than an hour before returning home.

Her phone was ringing as she unlocked the front door. It was Francisco, who apologized for not calling for the past couple of days. "As I said I might, I decided to take that cruise out to the Galapagos Islands," he explained. "That is definitely an experience I want to share with you. It's the kind of place you would love." Sabrina told him about Karenna's surprise visit, and Francisco was thilled to see positive progress in that relationship for Sabrina. They each told the other that they could barely wait for Francisco's plane to arrive the following week, and finally they reluctantly said good night.

That evening, Sabrina attended a Baha'i fireside nearby, taking along one of her new neighbors, Emily. Emily was the single woman in her early thirties who had recently left a job in advertising to open her own home based business as a gift basket entrepreneur. Throughout the speaker's presentation, Emily remained skeptical, but Sabrina participated animatedly in a discussion about the reality of the human soul. When they left, Sabrina was feeling a great excitement, but she saw that Emily did not share her enthusiasm, so she turned the conversation to Emily's business as they walked home. Emily explained that a younger brother had undergone chemotherapy when he was only twelve years old, and friends had made him a 'sunshine basket' which he had enjoyed opening, one gift at a time for days. Emily had realized that was a great business opportunity, and she now prepared gift baskets to mail all over North America, and she hoped to expand to Asia the following year.

"Wow, that's ambitious," Sabrina marveled. "How do you get your supplies?"

"The Internet. I think I keep FedEx in business," Emily laughed. "I'm making a fine living now, but I may expand some more. In that case, I'll have to rent warehouse space and hire staff. It's a tough decision. I like the thought of being an international company, but I'm not sure I'm willing to commit the time and money into growing bigger than I already am."

"You know, my husband did a lot of international work," Sabrina replied. "It really took a toll on him, and on us as his family, but that was because he was traveling so much. What you're talking about is buying product, storing it temporarily and rearranging it, then shipping it on to a new destination. You yourself, however, stay in the same physical place. It seems to me that your decision is about whether or not your added expenses will be offset by your sales growth, and also whether the additional time and effort will be worth the benefit."

"You sound like an MBA," Emily said enviously. "Where did you get that kind of knowledge?"

"Life," Sabrina answered seriously. "It's all about weighing options and making decisions."

"I guess you're right." By then they were back at their complex. "Thanks for inviting me tonight. I'd like to go again sometime, and maybe I'll pay better attention. Tonight my mind was a thousand other places."

"Any time you'd like. They have firesides at that home every Tuesday, and there is another location on Thursdays. We'd have to drive to that one, but I'd be glad to. Just let me know."

It was nearly 10:00 PM by the time Sabrina walked in her door. Having ignored the *Plain Dealer* that morning because of Karenna's arrival, she now sat down to glance through the paper before going to sleep. She scanned the front page, then flipped through the other sections. Suddenly she was riveted to a story that she re-read four times before throwing the paper to the floor. In terror, she flew to the front door to be sure it was double locked, then yanked the draperies across the sliding glass door at the back of the house. Still trembling, she crawled into bed fully clothed, and lay awake shaking all night.

NINETEEN

"He's *baaaack*," Sabrina was screaming into the telephone at 7:00 AM the next morning, as a dumbfounded Sally held the receiver as far from her ear as possible.

"Who's back? Francisco? I thought he wasn't coming until next week."

"Noo*oooo*. The devil. That bastard. The creature who ruined my life. He's back, and he did the same thing to two other women, only worse."

"Do you mean Bobby? Where did you see him? How do you know what he did?"

"I didn't see him," Sabrina screamed. "I read about it in the newspaper. He's on trial in Columbus, and he's just as smug as ever. His lawyer is claiming mistaken identity, and now both women are breaking down on their identifications. This can't be happening. It just can't." Sabrina was crying so hard she could no longer hold onto the telephone.

"I'm going to be at your house in one hour," Sally shouted over Sabrina's voice. "Just hang on. I'm on my way."

When Sally arrived, Sabrina had gotten herself under control, although barely. She was still wearing yesterday's clothes, had not washed her face, and had a haunted look that Sally had never seen. Sally wasn't sure what to do. Fearing that Sabrina was about to decompensate, she just said, "Tell me whatever you need to."

"Read that." Sabrina jabbed over and over at a newspaper clipping that had been torn out of the newspaper and thrown on the table. "Read it That will tell you everything.

Sally picked the mangled clipping up and slowly absorbed the story, while Sabrina paced. A Robert Evans was accused of raping two women in a small town outside of Columbus. One had been accosted on a jogging path, the other in a laundry room in the basement of an apartment building. Both had been blindfolded, trussed like pigs, and raped over and over for hours. Both had been severely beaten, then left for dead. The press was hailing their survivals as two separate miracles. One woman, an attorney, was now receiving long term disability payments because of irreversible brain damage. The other woman needed a wheelchair for mobility and could not speak. The trial hinged on debatable forensic evidence, and the defense attorney seemed to be winning.

"How do you know this is the same Robert Evans that you knew?" Sally asked. "That's a pretty common name."

"That's him," Sabrina answered defiantly. "I know it is."

"Even if it is, what can you do about it?" Sally was beginning to say more when Sabrina shrieked.

"I'm *responsible*. These women were injured because I was a coward. I should have stopped him."

"Sabrina, stop it. Right now, stop it." Sally commanded. "You are not responsible for what Bobby does. You had to protect Anna, and you did. That was your responsibility back then."

Sabrina blinked. After a moment she said, a bit more calmly, "Well, maybe that was my responsibility back then, but now is different. I can tell that court in Columbus what he did to me. Even if these women can't, I can. I wasn't hurt as badly as they were. My brain still functions."

"Sabrina, you're not thinking clearly. You're running on pure adrenaline right now. You can't make a decision that will affect so many people when you're in this state."

"*I'm* the one who's affected." Sabrina was growing angrier and angrier. "Why can't I make a decision for my own well being?"

"Because you have two children who don't know what

happened to you. Do you want them to read in a paper that their mother is testifying about being raped? You have to stop and think. Slow down."

That message forced Sabrina to cease pacing and sit down. "Of course. Yes. Paul. Karenna. My babies. I have to protect them."

"Sabrina, where are you?" Sally was beginning to feel hysterical herself. "Sabrina, look at me. Paul and Karenna are adults. You don't have any babies. Your children are grown."

Slowly, Sabrina stood up, walked to her bedroom and carefully sat down on the edge of her bed. "Sally, help me. I don't know what to do. I'm terrified. I've relived that night a thousand times in the last twelve hours. At one point, I would have shot myself if I had a gun in the house. I'm confused. I'm furious. I hurt so badly I want to rip my heart out. I can barely breathe. I . . ."

"All right. We're going to do things one at a time. First, I'm going to make you a sandwich. Then you're going to get some sleep. When you wake up, you're going to take a shower, and by then, I'll have a plan."

"Okay." Sabrina felt totally drained, like a transmission with a huge hole in it. "Peanut butter and orange marmalade, on rye."

After Sabrina had gone to sleep, Sally called a friend who was a therapist and got advice on what to do when Sabrina woke up. The friend counseled Sally to try to get Sabrina to a rape center, even if the occurrence had been a long time ago. There they could assess her condition and recommend a therapist to help her sort out the issues she had to deal with. Sally made several phone calls until she found the right organization. When Sabrina woke up, she gently guided her into agreeing to allow Sally to drive her to the clinic, and waited while she heard Sabrina sobbing and screaming and finally quieting down. The counselor at the clinic gave Sally an address and told her that an appointment had already been made for eight o'clock the following morning.

For three days, Sabrina talked with the therapist for hours at a time, until she finally began acting like the Sabrina that Sally knew. During this time, Sabrina stayed at Sally's home in order to intercept any telephone calls from Francisco. On the fourth day, Sabrina declared she was ready to call Francisco. When she reached him, she told him of her near collapse. Immediately, Francisco insisted on being there to help with her recovery. He arrived the following morning, two days earlier than planned, and found a hotel room nearby, fully understanding that this was not the time for physical intimacy.

Gradually, Sabrina began to think more clearly about

how to tell her children, and whether she should contact the prosecutor in Columbus. Francisco helped her through these agonizing choices, gently holding her hand and using his calming voice to steady her. Ultimately, Sabrina called the prosecutor and verified that this was indeed the same Bobby who had once lived in the same cities as she had. He was the right age, and when the prosecutor faxed her a picture, she recognized her tormentor instantly. The prosecutor told her that he was also a prime suspect in several other rapes dating back to the sixties. That revelation capped the decision for Sabrina, and she offered to be a witness. First, however, she told the prosecutor, she had to tell her family what had happened to her long before their own lives had begun.

She began by calling Karenna, who immediately offered to come back to Ohio to be with her mother throughout the ordeal of giving testimony in such a horrific case.

"Thank you, Sweetheart." Sabrina responded. "Your being with me would be so very, very welcome." Then she had explained that an old friend from college was with her. His name was Francisco, and she would tell Karenna more about him when she arrived.

Next she called Paul, which felt a lot harder to Sabrina, perhaps because he was male and might not understand the trauma so sensitively as Karenna immediately had. Paul, however, quickly grasped that his mother was suffering extraordinary pain. While he did not offer to come to the trial, he did ask his mother to call him to talk through whatever problems she had to deal with day by day. He congratulated Sabrina on choosing to seek a rape counselor, and related his own relief at talking through his long held fears and angers with a professional. "If only I had known," he said over and over. "I might still be married to my first wife Patricia, who loved me so much and I drove her away."

"Paul, darling, thank you so much for supporting me like this. I'm so sorry about Patricia. It's true that you can't go backward and undo old wrongs, but there is a whole exciting life to go forward toward. Please let yourself do that." Sabrina was startled to hear herself comforting someone else, and realized that her own healing had begun.

*   *   *

In Columbus, Sabrina and Karenna shared a hotel room, with Francisco next door.

Karenna had liked Francisco the instant she saw him, although she had been stunned to learn that her mother had had such a deep attachment to a man other than her own father. *Secrets, secrets,* Karenna kept thinking. When we believe we really know all about someone, how wrong we are. The dangers of premature judging applies to everyone, Karenna decided, even parents.

When Sabrina met the prosecutor, she was impressed with his relentless focus on convicting Robert Evans. His office had recently come across more definitive forensic evidence, and with that and Sabrina's testimony establishing a previous history of conduct, he was confident that he could achieve his goal of putting Robert behind bars for the rest of his life. "Three other women have come forward, as well as you," the prosecutor informed Sabrina. "They haven't yet committed to testifying, however."

"So there are at least six women whose lives this monster had destroyed," Sabrina retorted angrily. "All because I was too afraid to say anything. *Damn* me."

The prosecutor immediately corrected her. "You were not the first person Robert attacked. He frightened the others into silence, the same as he did to you. It started back when he was in high school. His behavior definitely is *not* your fault. You've been participating in counseling, so by now you know that." He looked at Sabrina with great compassion. "Don't allow him to continue controlling your life. Take the reins back into your own hands."

Sabrina shook with both fury and fear as she considered what could have happened to her when she was twelve years old. Thank God her family had moved when they did. But the prosecutor was right. She now understood that her destiny was within her own control, and she meant to assure that it stayed there.

"May I talk with the other women?" Sabrina asked. Perhaps if they felt that more people were joining together to confront Bobby . . . ah, Robert . . . they would feel safer."

The prosecutor was very pleased with this offer. "I'll see what I can arrange," he promised.

By the time Sabrina took the stand, there were seven women who testified to the horrors Robert Evans had committed, as well as four others who refused to come forward publicly, although they had given graphic accounts to the district attorney's staff. Robert Evans was convicted of multiple counts of rape, sodomy, kidnapping and assault. Months later he would be sentenced to life imprisonment without possibility of parole, although Sabrina only read about that in the paper. At his age, sixty-three, this seemed to be a punishment that in no way matched the magnitude of the crimes he had committed, but she drew some consolation from knowing that he could never assault another woman.

The experience of confronting Bobby had had profound effects on Sabrina, and she wasn't sure that she would ever plumb the depths of them all. Foremost for her, however, was how tragedy from the past had encouraged resolution of issues in the present. Those current issues were, she now realized, inextricably related to the past she had tried to force into non-existence. She and her children were now in regular, positive contact, which had at one time seemed an insurmountable task, and Sabrina finally acknowledged the link between the estrangement with her children and the events that had shut down her emotional functioning all those years before. Blessed Frank had tried so hard to bring her back to a happy life, even though he never knew the depth of what he was fighting against. He lost the battle because she was too afraid to share that moment of her life with her husband. *I'm sorry, Frank*, she sent heavenward again and again.

Karenna returned to Texas after the trial, and a few weeks later, called to tell Sabrina that she was pregnant again. Paul came to visit his mother at her new home, and Sabrina felt vindicated as she saw her son becoming the man she had always known was hidden deep within him. Paul had not yet established any long term relationship with another woman because this time, he assured his mother, he planned to know himself well enough to be able to provide a reliable partner for a woman. He still regretted that Patricia was no longer a part of his life, but she had long since re-married and moved on. Eventually, so would he.

After Sabrina returned to Cleveland, Francisco leased a

single family home a mile down the street from her condo. They shared keys to each other's residence, and it was if both of them had two homes. They would stay together at one place or the other most of the time, but occasionally Sabrina felt a need for independence and she would ask for a little time alone. Eventually Francisco came to accept this as part of who his beloved had become, and it no longer frightened him.

They traveled frequently. Sabrina loved the Galapagos as much as Francisco had anticipated she would, and Sabrina was delighted to share the majesty of the Grand Canyon with the man she considered her rock of stability. On their first trip to Peru, Sabrina was welcomed warmly by all of Francisco's family, and she finally felt a link in her life closing. They had taken Anna with them, and Sabrina was deeply touched by how Francisco's children treated her like their own aunt, with love and respect.

After several months, Sabrina realized that she was finally coming to grips with the realities of her relationship with Francisco del Oro. The luster of their first reunion had worn off, and they were now dealing with themselves as the adults they were today, not the lovers they had been in college. Both of them discovered habits in the other which set their teeth on edge, and it was welcome that they could pull back without pulling apart. Gradually they both came to realize that joining together two lives that had been so separate for so long was far more difficult than either of them had anticipated. For another six months they tried to determine whether or not they could live companionably into old age in one home, or each in their own space. Eventually they mutually agreed that living separately but very much together was the best arrangement for them both. Their deep and abiding love that had survived so much grew even stronger.

When Francisco's children and grandchildren came to visit from Peru, they did not crowd Sabrina, so she was able to enjoy participating in many of their activities while not feeling overwhelmed. Likewise, Paul and Karenna, who had become fond of the man whose existence had been kept from them but who had influenced their mother so greatly, insisted on including Francisco whenever they came to visit their mother.

Francisco and Sabrina grew old together, caring for one another through sickness and health while still respecting each other's need for time with their own families and for time alone. Francisco remained Catholic, and Sabrina continued to attend Baha'i firesides, with Francisco sometimes accompanying her but never becoming as devoted to the teachings of her new found faith as Sabrina was. Sally remained an integral part of their lives, as did Anna until she died in her mid-sixties. Sabrina and Francisco lived this combined yet separate lifestyle until Francisco passed away at the age of eighty-two. Sabrina then moved near Karenna's home in Texas, attended her three grandchildren's weddings, and became good friends with Paul's fourth and final wife. Sabrina lived to the age of ninety-four, and did not move to a nursing home until two months before her passing.